Mark O'Flynn was born in Melbourne and currently lives in the Blue Mountains. He began writing for the theatre and has had numerous plays professionally produced. He has also published a novella, a play, and two collections of poetry. His fiction and poetry have been published in a wide variety of journals and magazines in Australia and overseas. In 2001 he was a founding member of Weatherboard Theatre Company, and received funding from the NSW Ministry for the Arts to write *Eleanor & Eve*. This play was also staged by Railway Street Theatre in 2003.

Grassdogs was one of the winners of the Varuna Awards for Manuscript Development. Mark O'Flynn is married with two children.

MARK O'FLYNN

grassdogs

a novel

FOURTH ESTATE • *London, New York, Sydney* and *Auckland*

Fourth Estate
An imprint of HarperCollinsPublishers, Australia

First published in Australia in 2006
by HarperCollinsPublishers Australia Pty Ltd
ABN 36 009 913 517
www.harpercollins.com.au

HarperCollins*Publishers*
25 Ryde Road, Pymble, Sydney NSW 2073, Australia
31 View Road, Glenfield, Auckland 10, New Zealand
77–85 Fulham Palace Road, London W6 8JB, United Kingdom
2 Bloor Street East, 20th floor, Toronto, Ontario M4W 1A8, Canada
10 East 53rd Street, New York, NY 10022, USA

National Library of Australia Cataloguing-in-Publication data:

O'Flynn, Mark .
  Grassdogs.
  ISBN 978 0 7322 8334 6.
  ISBN 0 7322 8334 5.
  I. Title.
A823.3

Cover design by Greendot Designs Pty Ltd
Cover images: 'Primo' © Ken Shung, sky © Photolibrary, grass © Shutterstock
Typeset in 12pt/16pt ACaslon Regular by Helen Beard, ECJ Aust Pty Ltd
Printed and bound in Australia by Griffin Press on 70gsm Bulky Book Ivory

5 4 3 2 1   06 07 08 09

For Mick
and in memory of our brother Pete

Preliminary Submission

I am a man not persuaded much by landscape, although my mother has impressed on me that we each return to the earth from which we come. Or try to. Not that I have ever seen her pay much attention to the particular patch of earth from which she fled as soon as she was able. No, if there is anything to be learned here it is that one's parents are, in my opinion, usually mistaken about most things. Past is past. But misconceptions are hereditary, and the child will defend them in his blindness unto death. Being wrong does not mean being any less passionate about it.

I see I am covering too much ground.

To continue more simply:

I purr along the highway, changing gear on hairpin bends, the radio turned up loud. Trying not to think about my destination. Paying attention only to the road. I overtake trucks and Volvos. Nice to be out in the country, but that is all that is nice about it.

The Law has nothing to do with the truth, as Warren Pennington, senior partner with my firm, never tires of lecturing. The truth is malleable. And justice, like truth, is relative. Life is defendable, for a fee.

This is the man we have commissioned to free my uncle.

By the same token my mother never told me that I had an uncle until I was ten years old, and we were about to meet him. My feeling has always been that if they wanted to keep me in the dark then what should I care about the nature of their estrangements? Especially given what he was. In the Law and in the lounge room, secrecy and subterfuge are the norm.

I pull into the car park, find a space, and listen to the ticking of the motor beneath the bonnet. I am early. I watch the gate open and a white truck come out. At the foot of the great, grey wall not a blade of grass is growing. The grass has been banished to the far side of the car park. I open the file lying on the passenger seat and on top of the brief is a newspaper photo of my uncle. Our Client.

I do not particularly care that I have an uncle. The one my father refers to by the solitary syllable, 'Hmph'. His opinion has never really counted for much. When you live in different cities the distance is more than geographical. I know the myth, but I do not bother myself with the reasons why my mother ran away from home to the anonymous haven of the city. It is her business. As my life is mine. If it has been her ambition to give me the upbringing she herself has not received, then, well and good. I have not asked for it. I take everything as my due. I am sure I would have thrived on neglect as much as on the honesty of her poverty.

I was born with the common congenital deformity of the hard palate in the roof of my mouth. By all accounts the nasal septum and vomer bone are absent and the first eighteen months of my infancy can be regarded as a clinical affair. All this is hearsay, of course, as there are no photographs of me as a baby in existence. (Wouldn't want Emily to get hold of those.) My mother never speaks to me of it, for which I have been grateful. The wonders of modern medicine have rectified all trace of any abnormality and I recall nothing of the remedial speech training I later received. All that thriving. The only repercussion now is that I must be careful when swimming in chlorinated water (I was a grommety kid), although I have never explained why this is to Emily. She simply thinks I am a very kissable bad swimmer, and God knows, she says, there's room enough in this world for bad swimmers as well as good. Anyway, swimming is not something a busy young solicitor with a demanding schedule has a lot of time for. There is no catharsis here, I hope —

But I see I am covering too much ground again.

I close the car door and it beeps its locks at me. I march across the concourse in my suit.

Back then, in Melbourne, living on the meagre, single wage of my father, Gordon Tindale, my parents must have spent years under not inconsiderable financial strain.

In the gatehouse an officer stares at me through thick perspex. I state my business. I hand over my keys and mobile phone. Someone comes out to muss through the papers in my briefcase. I sign in, and print in the visitors' book the name of the inmate I am here to see. The heavy, steel door springs open with an electronic whine. Is this my luminous vision?

Seven months ago, my mother flew up to see me with the unwelcome memory of an uncle I have met but once (do I remember?) who now needs my help. Who? She has a file of newspaper clippings. How can I help?

By paying attention, she says.

She also has a history in which I should have a vested interest, in a landscape as new to me as the moon; the foreign earth from which she came.

Now I pass through the gate. I begin to pay attention.

ONE

The mother's silky was the first. Its ears full of grass seeds. Then he could remember a waddling Labrador that adopted him. The father's kelpies and cattle dogs, Rex and Bex, or the parents of Rex and Bex, rattling their chains in their drums. One by one the dogs came. They gathered together in the mother's decrepit house, which nestled in a dish scooped out of the earth that could not be called a valley, beyond the desolate edge of one town, before the ragged council fringes of the next.

After the father's death, the nameless farm, which had been a burden to them always, was whittled down to feed the parasites of bankers. Good riddance, said the mother, in time. They would survive on air and eggs. Only rats would flee the sinking ship.

In time all they were left with was the weatherbeaten house, smooth as driftwood, with its raw boards surrounded by grass, baking under the sun. A few acres, gnawed to the roots. All that thrived were weeds. And dogs. These acres were the only buffer between the world he knew and the encroaching universe that was Dungay's farm. On the other side of the boundary fence, Dungay's sheep were fat — they did not get braxy, his canola grew tall and yellow as the sun, his cows did not get bloat. The air over his earth smelled rich with superphosphate.

Fences meant nothing to the boy, Edgar. To him the world was green and limitless. The old combine harvester in its shed, full of mice, rusting into the ground, was like a statue in a temple. Earth was earth, whether it was on this side of the fence or the other. A wonder to behold, and sometimes, when he was an infant, he would stuff fistfuls of it into his mouth.

His mouth.

When the harvester was gone, taken by the re-possessors, the shed was still a temple only bigger. Thin straws of sunlight dropped down from empty nailholes in the roof like filaments of web, or shadows of swirling light in a river. As he grew, Edgar liked to spend time in there, doodling in the dust, or hunting mice, until one or other of the dogs came to lick his hand. The father, Alf, whose roles as farmer and provider had been taken from him, shooed the boy out into the fresh air so that he could be alone in his great empty shed. Edgar would sneak in later to see what he'd been up to and find piles of crooked nails arranged into circles, or two spanners leaning against each other for balance. And the growing stack of empty bottles. Edgar could understand the attraction of the shed, where such things could be accomplished. Sometimes the father even slept out there, muttering to himself in the darkness. The dogs followed Edgar, who learned how to roam at a young age. Those animals had been farm dogs — Rex and Bex, good solid work dogs with nothing now to do. Of course they would follow him. Edgar was the most active thing in their lives. They taught him curiosity, and Edgar had not a moment's tedium in his boyhood.

Part of what he ran from was their arguing. The perpetual squabbling which would sometimes descend into violence. The mother gave as good as she got, and once Edgar saw her tip a mug of steaming tea on the father's snoring head. The house dog yapped madly, dancing between their fumbling struggle, and the father booted it across the room.

The mother kept her silky terrier inside with her. Its hair was a beautiful blend of blue-black and sandy-brown, which matched a memory Edgar had of the father's own hair. There must have been more than one house dog, for Edgar recalled that there had always been a silky. The stay-at-home dog. It would sleep in Edgar's lap until his legs grew numb.

The mother baked scones. She smelled of flour.

If, during his roaming, Edgar skinned his knee or stubbed a toe he would get the dogs to lick it. They seemed to like this and lined up to take turns. The mother said it was disgusting, the way he took after the father. He'd get germs. He'd get gangrene, or catch a parasite. She wished them out of her kitchen and quick-sticks about it, waving a wooden spoon like a sceptre. It sounded like much else of her hollow way of speaking to him, which he didn't understand. And he'd bolt.

For those who like omens, even Edgar's birth foretold the trouble he would come to cause. The mother's labour pains began prematurely. The father was spraying in the top paddock. Thinking they were Braxton Hicks contractions, the mother carried on working. Soon it became obvious they were not. She called but no one came. By the time Alf got back to the house, the mother was half-conscious on the kitchen floor in a pool of amniotic fluid, covered in a dusting of flour. Alf bundled her into the ute and sped to the Base Hospital, forty minutes away in the big city of Wagga. A bit of the umbilical cord was already protruding. The amnion had ruptured. Fathers in those days ('Thank Christ') were not permitted to watch a caesarean section. Even though butchering a heifer was next to nothing. It was much safer to pace the floor. In addition the cord was tight about the infant's neck, his head bluer than the rest of the blue body, mottled with meconium. The doctor feared he was stillborn, but as he cut away the cord the baby squawked — through, they all now saw, a gaping cleft palate. Perhaps, the father thought, it might have been better had he been lost: give the kid a dong on the noggin, like an unwanted kitten. But Edgar was resilient. In fact, after his shaky start, he thrived. He was a weed. He lived on nothing. Everyone found reasons to blame themselves. Alf, for instance, who never grew used to looking at the mouth, saying it was all his fault and the kid was the result of a drunken fuck.

Father Fletcher wanted to baptise the boy, but Alf would not let him.

The surgery that followed a few years later was, unlike mine, less than successful. The cleft palate was incompletely repaired, leaving Edgar with a great weal in his lip that dominated not only his face, but his whole way of speaking and confronting the world.

At least, the father used to say, pacing the kitchen, it was a damn sight better than the little turnip-headed gargoyle they had brought home from the hospital, who didn't stop drooling.

'I coulda done a better job meself with a bit of baling twine,' he used to say of the son who would one day inherit the farm.

Edgar had a dim memory of the family sitting around the table in the kitchen. Had there always been just the three of them? Weren't there more? Moths tapped at the window. Edgar threw food for the silky. The parents were talking about him. He knew this by their tone, the occasional glances, and the words that buzzed and hissed and clicked in his ears like the sounds of insects. He looked at their mouths moving, pieced together the sounds which tumbled out. The father sometimes stood behind the highchair and clapped his hands loudly. Edgar would not scare.

Edgar ate moths. He ate dirt. Once he ate a mouse. When they laced gloves to his little wrists he gnawed them off. They gave up slapping his hands. The growling sound that said '*don't*' was, he thought for a long time, his name. Needless to say he loved his parents, as he loved the silky and the others. Once, as they ate silently at their wooden table, the mother suddenly jumped to her feet coughing hideously. She tried riotously to pound her own back. Gagged for some water.

'A bit of pepper on the old tonsil,' she managed to say hoarsely, her face purple.

The mother's fit subsided. Edgar's father turned to him.

'Let that be a lesson to yer, Ed my lad, never marry a woman unless yer can stand ter watch 'er chokin' with a bit of pepper on 'er tonsil.'

The mother guzzled at the tap.

'Thanks for nothin', yer great lummox.'

Whenever the father toured the paddocks, or even travelled into town in the old ute, it was a treat for Edgar to be allowed to sit up on the tray with the work dogs. If he ever fell off, bumping over ditches, the father would say:

'It ain't no picnic for me either, son.'

Soon the father whistled him up there with the dogs when work was done. Edgar would look back in wonder along the line of freshly cut hay, bound and scattered like building bricks, or coiled up like a cake shop of snails. He learned to keep his balance and not fall off. There seemed to be the joy of contest up there with the dogs, the wind in their open mouths. Edgar hung on tight. He had the better of them. He was their master.

In town he would stay up on the tray while the parents disappeared into the supermarket, or the hardware-and-farm supplies, or the bank, or the hotel, or any number of other businesses. All these things he had to learn about. Some days they spent a lot of time inside. Others, a short time. Edgar was not very good at knowing how much time had passed. He could, however, sense a change in their mood, their state of mind when they emerged from these businesses, although he did not know what these states of mind might mean. From the supermarket, laden with shopping bags, they seemed resolute, fortified. From the bank they emerged miserable, angry. They seemed happiest when they burst from the pub, staggering with bottles that they dumped in the back with him. He did not know the songs that they sang:

'A-hubba hubba hubba, a-hello Jack
A-hubba hubba hubba, I just got back
A-hubba hubba hubba, a-whadda you know?
It was mighty smoky over Tokyo.'

He watched them collapse into the front seat of the cabin, their laughter suddenly cut short by the doors. Search and fumble for the keys. He saw the strange looks the dogs gave both of them through the back window, ears cocked, heads on one side, trying to make a little sense of the world.

One day, after the windy drive to town, as they waited parked in the street, Edgar jumped out of the ute. The sky did not darken. The ground did not open up. He wandered to the corner, then wandered back. The blue heeler, Rex, remained in the back, still loyal to the father, standing on an old tarpaulin. The earth did not tremble. Edgar wandered in the other direction, gauging his distance from the ute. He found a cake shop and gazed in the window. The town was filled with noise and turbulence. The first time he heard a siren he ran back to the ute and took his cue from the dogs by hiding under the tarp. There was so much going on. It was infectious, the buzzing language of the town. The cars that hissed past on the wet street. His reflection in shop windows as he marched by. The armless, naked mannequins being clothed in the dress shop windows. He stopped and stared until a woman in the window flapped her hand at him irritably. But Edgar was not staring at their nudity, which was more akin to udders at milking time. He was staring at their smooth limblessness. He wondered if his own severed arms would look so pure.

He loved the smells of the cake shop best. He moved on until he came to a building he had seen in passing but never taken much notice of before. Nor had he ever seen the parents enter it. What funny business went on in there? A sign which he could not read proclaimed: *Jesus Saves*. He heard robust music. The big wooden doors were not locked. Inside it was dark and cavernous, like the empty shed at home. He noticed the stained-glass windows, covered from the outside by wire mesh. Pictures of naked babes with sparrow wings. Ox hearts. He smelled the candlewax. Walking quietly up the aisle he was startled by a young man with a whiskered dimple in his chin, who emerged from a side door and stared at him.

'Hailyoungfellow. Whatdoyouwant? Areyoulost?'

Edgar said nothing. He did not fully understand the man's words, but he understood the tone. It was the warning growl of ownership over a morsel when another dog comes too close. The man pressed a button on the tape deck hidden in the shadows and the music stopped.

'Speakupboy,' taking a step, 'Whathappened toyourface? Comehereintothelight.'

Edgar was fast. He was outside, slowing to a walk in the sunshine before the man growled out something else from the doorway. Edgar looked back with perfect confidence in the abilities of his own body.

Just along the street Edgar was surprised to find, sitting there on the footpath, a bucket of food. Good smells came from it. He parted some of the papers with his hands to find out what it was. It was half a lamington. He looked up and two boys his own size were standing staring at him. He had the lamington in his hands.

'You're a dirty pig,' said one.

'You're a spaz,' said the other.

'Lookit his gob.'

'What a pig.'

Edgar stamped his foot, as if to take a step towards them, but they sauntered off, equally confident, looking back at him.

'Hail, fellows.'

The priest in the doorway stood aside to let them enter.

'Good morning, Father Fletcher.'

'Do you know that boy?'

'No, Father Fletcher.'

'He looks familiar.'

'No Father.'

They glanced at Edgar, before the man eased the wooden door shut. In a while the sound of singing started again. Edgar ate.

* * *

Back at the ute the parents still had not returned. The world did not end. Time had stopped still. The dogs were glad to see him and smell him as he clambered into the back. They laid their cold noses against his skin. Soon enough, in the distance he saw the parents staggering towards them.

'A–hubba hubba hubba, a–hello Jack . . . '

He learned in that moment that his life was his own, that with this independence, consequences only applied if he was caught, and in this way he was able to uncover the strange pattern to the town. The dogs were silent in their conspiracy. The parents, after tossing their supplies into the back with barely a word to Edgar, fell laughing into the cabin.

'Yer great lummox.'

'Yer great heifer.'

'Bag yer head, yer drongo.'

'Bag yer own.'

It had been a good afternoon. As they pulled out of the carpark he found the biscuits and shared them with the dogs. Consequences often came too late for the lesson to be learned.

The wind flung Edgar's hair about and dried out his tongue. At speed he could not face directly into the wind the way the dogs could. They enjoyed it. The father had told him if he was thirsty then he should suck a stone, one from the river, nice and cool. Edgar had a couple in his pocket for this purpose. Also for pinging at birds or other targets. Smooth pebbles of quartz that felt snug in his hands and in his mouth. There was nothing so useful as a stone.

He loved the sound of the tyres rumbling over the bitumen, the tilt of the ute as they braked into curves. Peering over the edge at how the wheels spun, how the rubber pancaked on the road, he could tell if one had more or less air in it than the others. As they left the precinct of the town proper, turning off the Sturt, down the Olympic Way, Edgar looked for, and found in the distance the familiar silhouette of the Rock, lying along the horizon like a sleeping beast. The Rock was the only feature in their landscape which could approximate a landmark, although to Edgar the clumps of trees, the corrugated furrows of the paddocks, the passage of seasons, and smells, were all as good as landmarks.

The Rock in the distance resembled the crouching outline of a lion, or else, Edgar preferred to think, a dog. The sphinx, although only the father had seen photos of the sphinx. It was too small for a mountain; however, in relation to the placid ripples of the bountiful farmland hereabouts (most people just said it was flat), the Rock took on the proportions of a mountain.

Many times around the table, the silky asleep on a mat by the Bega Meters combustion stove, Edgar listened to the father retell the story of the Rock. How the crows came from its nether regions; and this being a district of crows, even a farm boy could see the importance of that. The blacks called it Kengol and did their funny business up on it at night. How, in those distant days, the sphinx had once possessed a head, giving it an even more prominent lion-like outline, and had gone by the name of Hanging Rock. Who had they hanged there? the son wondered. Morgan the bushranger was said to have used it as a lookout, and sheltered in its caves. Leaning back in his chair, hands clasped behind his shaggy head, the father told how his father, or his father's father, or someone's father had, in the spirit of sons, broken into the shed one heated evening after shearing. How a mate, let's call him Davo, stood cockatoo and bore witness. How they took the dynamite and detonators and all the other accoutrements that go with dynamite: a case of longnecks, matches, and enough ambition to get them through the night. Did they pedal? Or did they take the sulky and old Dobbin? Or did they grind close together in a single saddle? It would have been a dirt road in those days. It certainly weren't no picnic. Alf's chair creaked. By hook or by crook they made their way to the base of Hanging Rock. A township had sprung up there. A butcher's. A red-brick School of Arts hall. A line of bird-filled trees spaced up the wide main street, thriving in the heat of those summers, much hotter than what pass for summers these days. It was an hour's climbing up the winding, narrow track, through hissing she-oaks, to the top. And at night? Even longer. Easy to lose the track. In the moonlight the shadows of the surrounding hills, particularly the ridge falling gently to the south, wormed their way into the distance like a great vein beneath the earth. The stars much brighter than the stars we get these days. After sweating their way to the top the farm boys lay and drank. Edgar's father leaned back and drank. Edgar heard the bubbles rise in his throat. Did he mention it was New Year's Eve? Did he mention the year was 1899? Or was it just the 1870s? No — the end of the old century, one of sweat and toil, sounded much more plausible. Whose father was it again? Edgar looked at the father telling the story as if it had been him doing the climbing, the drinking. They planted the dynamite in crevices and cracks about the lion's neck. A precipitous cliff dropped beneath them. They lay back and waited, counting down the century on a silver watch borrowed from Davo's old man. No lights of distant station houses pricked the darkness. They drank the warm grog. Eventually they struck their wax-coated matches and scampered across the rocks, down their planned escape route as fast as their drunken stumblings would let them. They hid behind some boulders. Waiting. They had forgotten the watch. Where was it? They looked up at the lion's head, hanging out over the precipice, dark against the purple night sky. Had the fuse gone out? Go and check. No, you. Did one stand up? Poke his head above the ledge of their shelter? The explosion rent the night. The sound of crows erupted upward. Rocks and stones rained down. Did they embrace? Did they sing *Auld Lang Syne*? No one knew if they had timed it for exactly midnight. Apart from some splintered trees and the obvious decapitation, the small rock-fall left no sign of itself. The cloud of dust soon settled. The farm boys went home. The following year they said it rained fish.

So the farm boys blew the hanging bit off Hanging Rock. In the logical light of a new century, and amid the repercussions for the act which have long since faded, Hanging Rock became known simply as 'the Rock'. The scar in the earth was soon thick with regrowth. A new path had to be negotiated, but really, when you glanced at the view, for that was all it was worth, there was not much to look at. Wheat silos were built. The rail siding. More butchers. Bakers. The sun beat down upon them all during those relentless summers. Everyone prospered.

Edgar looked at the father. Had he prospered? Where was this prosper? His father blew his lips and made a squeaking noise. He scratched his jowls, kicking off his boots into a corner of the kitchen.

'Let this be a lesson to yer, my lad, not to go drinkin' warm grog.'

Was this man his father? Was it really just the three of them? What happened to the farm boys? Edgar hoped they got away with it, that they had copped no more than a hiding. And was this really the reason there were so many crows about?

The mother piped up from the stove:

'Stop fillin' that boy's head up with stuff and nonsense, and git yer feet off the bloody table.'

And the father did.

As he grew, Edgar climbed the Rock many times. Each time with a different dog, but always a dog. He climbed the spine of the lion, adding his tracks to an unformed trail. The main track wound up the forelimbs and shoulders of the beast. He discovered and explored the series of caves in the ridge which stood like a stone wave extending south from the lion's forepaws. Maybe Morgan the bushranger had camped here. Maybe not. He knew every crevice and chink in the Rock. Or so he felt. The red-capped robin, the brown tree-creeper. Even down to the dams and the haystacks on the plains below, which crept right to the flanks of the monolith. That was the father's word, *monolith*, like your head.

He remembered the father telling versions of the story at the bar of the Quinty, beneath the leathery heads of a brace of gaping Murray cod nailed to the wall, his audience also yawning.

Edgar camped and hunted and built forts on the Rock. He caught skinks and kept them for a while in a tin before releasing them. The dogs watched him curiously and sometimes Edgar asked them in his father's voice to pass the spanner or the hammer or the salt. He accumulated stones and spent hours in target practice. He piled seven or eight rocks on top of each other in a tall cairn he did not understand. He loosened other boulders and took great pleasure in watching them tumble and crack and echo down the flanks of the Rock, smashing through woolly ears of ragwort. He listened intently until long after the crashing sounds of trees fending the boulders off faded away.

For a certain breed of boy, left to his own devices, it was a type of idyll.

On one of his expeditions his dog paused, hackles erect at a low-slung fringe of she-oaks. There amongst the carpet of needles was a trapped fox. Its front leg broken in the trap's clenched grin. The dog's lip was curled back over its teeth, growl low in its throat. The fox barely had strength to lift its head. Edgar examined it closely, keeping a firm stick in his hand. Was he putting his face too close to the muzzle of the fox? Suddenly it bucked with its final instinct and seized Edgar's arm, its needle fangs piercing his shirt and the skin within the shirt.

Edgar cried out: 'Sick 'im, dorg.'

Rex — or was it Bex? — leapt on the fox's throat as Edgar tore his arm free. Soon it was a dead fox. Edgar gripped his arm and fell back as the dog shook the limp fox in its jaws. The trap jangled and seemed to be alive. He used his torn shirt to wrap his arm before he called the dog off.

'Good dorg, good dorg,' he patted it. Pain burned in his arm. Edgar took the wadding of his shirt away and was interested to watch the blood well from the puncture marks in his flesh. If he clenched his fist the blood welled faster. Pain flashed to his shoulder. When it subsided he wondered if he should take the brush as a souvenir. It was pretty mangy. He turned back down the track, his arm pulsing at each step. The dog bounding ahead, and then back, to hurry him along. When they reached the bottom they rested. His arm throbbed. Edgar found movement more comfortable. If he sat down he would never want to get up again. The pain urged him on. From behind the Rock in raggedy formation above him, like car doors opening and closing, came the proverbial croaking of crows.

The father gripped his arm in his hands and studied the wound. A flap of skin hung loosely between two gouges. The bleeding was slow to stop. He cuffed Edgar gently over the side of the head. The mother washed the wound and wrapped up ice in a bit of linen and made him hold it against the broken skin. He wanted her to hold him, but there was drinking to be done. That night he heard them again arguing over their clinking bottles. He knew it was about him, even though the words were no more than a buzz through the walls. The boy was always doing things like this. How many shirts was she expected to mend? Then don't mend them. When the pain was too great they gave him a glass of brandy, which burned his throat, but finally made him go asleep where he dreamed of the father sitting at the end of the bed, watching over him.

In all this, school had been a fleeting abstraction in Edgar's experience. His memory of it was limited. Children laughed and sniggered on the bus. No one wanted to sit near him. He was confronted in the playground by the two churchboys who had accosted him on the streets of town. They liked him even less than when they recalled him burrowing about in a bin. They told everyone. The girls stared in revulsion. They swung their plaits and pinched their noses. Someone accused him of looking at her underpants. He was reprimanded by the principal. The teacher, in a placatory role, swiftly learned to ignore him. Edgar remained quiet in class and stared out the window at birds; at a tractor mowing the oval; at the arc of the sun. If they did not want him here, then why was he here? If he spoke they all laughed. One girl in particular took pity on him, so it seemed. Her name was Ivy Cornish and she spoke to him in the playground, where the asphalt basketball court radiated the lunchtime heat. He sat on the hard ground, panting a little. He was having trouble undoing the plastic wrap of his sandwiches. The girl approached and asked his name. Edgar noticed the ribbons in her hair, their baubles.

'Ed,' he told her, 'Edgar Hamilton.'

She took his sandwiches and unwrapped them. She was an expert.

'I'm Ivy Cornish,' said Ivy Cornish. 'My father owns Cornish's Newsagency. Where do you live?'

'I live —'

Before he could finish a group of girls floated their laughter across the basketball court. One of them, he knew, was called Sophie Trelawney. All the boys liked her. She was the sister of one of the Sunday school boys. Sophie and Ivy. He looked at Ivy's pretty face, its splash of freckles. Was she hiding a smile? Had Sophie dared her to come and speak to him? Were they trying to imagine what he might say? Edgar thought he could smell her toothpaste. A boy called Doug Medson wandered past bouncing a ball.

'What are you talkin' to that halfwit for?'

''Cause I wanna,' Ivy Cornish snapped back.

'If you talk to that spaz, then you're a spaz.'

The boy moved on and Ivy Cornish returned to Sophie and her friends. Giggling Gerties, the mother would have called them. Trumped-up little sluts, the father. Edgar did not know what those things were. They were just things parents said, which stuck in his mind like grains of glass. ('Life's a bucket full of nuts and bolts, my lad,' the father said, 'but it's still got a bloody great hole in it, and at the end of the day there's just nuts.') Sometimes he sat next to Ivy Cornish in class and she whispered the answers to him, but still he got them wrong. The teacher made Ivy move away from him. In the playground he heard the boys, egged on by Doug Medson, singing:

Ivy's in the cellar
By Glory can't you smell her
With snot *dribbling down her nose*
Dribbling down her nose to her toes.'

When Edgar found Ivy crying behind the toilets he felt a surge of anger rise through him. Edgar had a feeling that made his bowels go hot and watery. He became aware of a defence more powerful than indifference. He had an ally. He wanted to smash those kids, although it felt strange, perhaps unnatural, not to be the focus of their derision. He wanted to help her. He would do anything for her to prove his loyalty. But she did not want his loyalty. When Ivy looked up and saw him she ran away.

Sometimes Sophie Trelawney asked him what kind of cheese he ate. Edgar knew whatever answer he gave would be wrong. There were other rhymes for him. Sophie chewed her nails to the quick. Or was it Ivy? They were best friends. He liked them both but they didn't need him. Sophie showed him how to write his own name, but when he tried to copy the letters she formed, all he was able to conjure was *Ebgr Ham*. Nevertheless, he would have a long memory of her ravaged fingers as they held the crayon which formed the swoop of her *S*'s, like the path of a bird in flight. Edgar started chewing his nails too.

Another time, it might have been the same day for all Edgar knew of time, he found himself within the rich aromas of the school toilet block. Such smells and sounds among the dribbling cisterns, the flushings, the footsteps in and out. Edgar was hiding in the cubicle where it was quiet. No one could find him here. At his feet, between his shoes, lay half a broken razor blade. He recognised it as an instrument to do with fathers. What was it doing here on the toilet floor? It was brown and rusty and cold. He turned it in his fingers. He heard footsteps slap into the toilet block and step up to the urinal. Edgar peered beneath the cubicle door. It was Doug, the boy who'd called him *spaz*, who had insulted Ivy for talking to him. Edgar recognised the boy's smell. The boy shook himself energetically as Edgar stole from the cubicle. He crept up behind, holding the broken razor blade, and slashed twice, deeply, down the back of the boy's bare knee. The boy screeched, and hobbled in pain and fear away from Edgar.

Edgar followed him out into the sunshine where the children ran away and the grown-up-on-duty was obliged to intervene.

He could not remember the look on the boy's face. He could not remember the words the teacher, and later the principal used on him, apart from one which was:

'Typical.'

In fact he could not remember his teacher at all. When he tried to climb out the window during his interrogation, they seized him. Edgar bit and thrashed at them, kicking over a chair. He rather liked the noise the chair made. They held him until the father arrived. Smirked when they saw the battered ute pull into the school grounds. Hadn't they been told a hundred times not to smirk? The father hurled Edgar about the room, until the principal asked him to desist from corporal punishment and instead to remove his son from the premises. ('Listen, boxhead, no one tells me how to discipline my son.') The father hauled Edgar by the scruff of the neck out of the office, and the building, slamming doors, bellowing as he went: 'Is that how yer keep yer dignity, is it?' and tossed him into the back of the ute where he sat in the sun, contented. The son did not remember the words the father used when they got back home, or the lashings of the belt, confused as they were with all the other lashings. He realised, once his abrasions healed, that his time with school was over. The glimmer of this dawning filled him like a glass with honey, with a golden liberation.

Edgar worked the farm with the father. He trained the dogs and rode with them in the back of the ute. His body grew strong, his bones firm. His knowledge of the world instinctive and ruled by reflex. Years later, the truant officer came to the farm, knocking loudly at the doors and windows. He walked about the house peering in. The silky yapped. The mother finally relented and opened the door, giving Edgar the chance to skip out the back. He jumped the yard fence and, in the company of dogs, whose chains he loosened at the tank, ran over the fresh furrows of the paddocks towards the Rock. The green stalks of wheat fell beneath his feet.

He knew no truant officer, or anyone, would ever find him. He was big. He was strong. He knew things. He was faster than even the father. He ate fruit and vegetables plucked from Dungay's house garden, surprised at the colour of unearthed carrots.

He made a hidey-hole in one of Dungay's perfect haystacks and slept there comfortably, huddled with his dogs for warmth. He listened to the postman's farting motorbike delivering Dungay's mail.

He thought he was in for another hiding when cold drove him home two days later, but the father was catching up on his ploughing, and the mother was humming in the kitchen. Her spirits had been rejuvenated in his absence, though when she saw him, she gave him a hug, absentmindedly, smelling of dough and sherry, inspecting his shirt and patting his head.

'Good boy . . . Down now.'

Edgar had no need to think beyond the pleasures of each minute. It was the father who insisted he try to think ahead to next year's harvest, sowing, scarifying; the future needs of the soil.

'Gotta think ahead, me boy. Hold yer head up.'

Alf thought of nothing else, burdened as he was by his debts. Forget the past. But that year he had to sell the tractor and the seeder and spent more time in his shed than ever.

When Sophie Trelawney disappeared there was a terrible outcry in the district and the town. Edgar had all but forgotten her. Who? He recalled that she wore her hair in plaits. Concern grew to fear, and soon to panic. Stormwater drains leading to the river were untangled and searched. The river was dragged by a launch with police divers sifting through the mud and willow roots on the bottom. Nothing.

A small mannequin dressed in the clothes in which Sophie was last seen was placed at the entrance of the supermarket. Edgar did not recognise the mannequin. The father hurried him on to the ute.

Fear turned to hysteria. Mr and Mrs Trelawney begged on the television. Days went by. Father Fletcher offered up a mass. It seemed everyone knew someone from the district who was questioned. To object invited suspicion. But it was still a surprise when the hare-lipped boy from her primary school days — what was their relationship again? — was taken in for questioning.

Actually they came out to the farm, two detectives in suits, and found Edgar and his dad at sullen work in their shed beside the lacerated shade of the peppercorn tree. Edgar tracing the flight of birds, the *S*'s that Sophie had taught him, in the dust with a stick. The father had long given up trying to get a sensible conversation out of the boy.

'Alf?'

A great gash of sunlight in the door.

'Who's asking?'

'Detective Gould, and this is Detective Tavistock. We want to ask you about the young girl, Sophie Trelawney.'

'I heard about that. You haven't found her, then?'

'No, we haven't.'

'So what are you doing?'

'We're looking.'

Edgar looked at them from a circle he had drawn around himself in the dust.

'I bet you are.'

'What do you mean by that, Alf?'

'What makes you think she might be here?'

'Since you know what we're talking about, you wouldn't happen to know the whereabouts of Sophie Trelawney?'

'Nope.'

Alf whacked at a piece of metal stuck in a vice.

'I beg your pardon?'

'Nope, I fucking wouldn't.'

'There's no need to take that tone.'

'This is my fuckin' property. I'll take whatever tone I like.'

Edgar saw the hairs on his father's knuckles. *Whack whack.*

'Things must be pretty desperate.'

'They haven't taken me house yet.'

'Well, Alf, they seem to have taken everything else.'

'Pissorf.'

The police were very patient. The second one was staring firmly at Edgar. Rex sat beside him in the dirt. Sunlight from the holes where the rivets had rusted through.

'We understand that Sophie was friends with a lass called Ivy Cornish, who knew your son. We have information that he once tried to pull down her underwear.'

There was a pause. All three men fixed their eyes on Edgar.

'It's him we'd actually like to talk to, Alf,' said the other. 'We're questioning everyone.'

'Well yer can't.'

'Why not?'

''Cause lookit him, he ain't got the brains of a rissole.'

'He's a big strong lad.'

'And he was here any night you care to mention.'

'Which night was that?'

'Any night you care to mention.'

'He's not under suspicion, Alf, we simply want to rule him out of our inquiries.'

'Well, yez can fuckorf out of my shed,' the father raised his voice, 'and yez can fuckorf of my property.'

'Alf, we'll simply get a warrant.'

'Get what yez like, but I'll meet yez at the gate.'

'What do you say, lad?' They turned to Edgar, but Edgar said nothing.

The detectives looked closely at the father and at Edgar, before walking out of the shed. The father flung a spanner after them which clanged against the corrugated iron. The dust hanging in the still air. He looked at Edgar as though he was about to make another of his pronouncements. *There son, that's how yer deal with scummy fuckers that want yer balls. That's how yer keep whatever shitty little bit of dignity yer got left.* But he said nothing, and his breathing rasped and echoed in the hollow shed.

The mother smelled of dough and sherry.

She cleaned her fingernails with a broken match.

She hummed along to the wireless.

She spoke fondly of 'Blue Hills' by Gwen Meredith.

She hated the news and knew in advance when to turn the wireless off.

She cleaned her ear by wiggling the tip of her little finger in it.

She had no photographs of herself.

She had a silky-haired terrier that she loved.

She quilted bedspreads.

She knitted jumpers.

She counted the stitches.

She had blue eyes.

She was not fat.

She liked baking.

She had long hair which she kept tied up in a bun.

She chuckled like a gang-gang parrot.

She could not drive.

She had red hair.

She had once been proposed to at a bush dance by a man named Clifford Bull.

She liked to sit on the porch and slap flies.

She liked sherry.

She went with the father when he was taken in for questioning.

She hated mosquitoes.

She lived in the Riverina all her life.

She had never climbed the Rock.

She grew old suddenly after she found the body of the father and the rifle near him in the empty shed.

She would not speak to Father Fletcher.

She hugged Edgar to her skirts.

Her red hair turned grey. Grey turned her clothes.

She stopped her knitting.

She liked sherry.

She fed the silky the best cuts of meat.

She spent longer on the porch.

She fed stale scones to the chickens.

She did not chase Edgar any more when he left the house.

She did not ask where he had been when he returned.

Her name was Mrs Hamilton.

Edgar watched the body of the father, covered in a sheet, wheeled on a gurney to the back of the ambulance. Sunset bleeding over the stubble of wheat. The stretcher's legs folded up like an ironing board. One by one the cars left. The police. The neighbours. The welfare people. Was there anyone who could come to stay with Mrs Hamilton to look after the boy? No sister, or relative? No, there was no one. When they were finally alone, the mother closed the door to her room and lay down on the big bed. Edgar heard her crying to herself. '*Nnn, nnn, nnn.*' The rhythm of her sobs had a stamina in it, like a parrot, as if it were conserving energy to last all night. The silky scratched at the door and Edgar heard her shuffling footsteps, heard the door open a fraction to admit the dog. He glimpsed her wan, desolate face. He went out to the big shed under its powerful tang of pepper, and looked at all the footprints in the dust.

I, Tony Tindale, did not choose to be involved in this avuncular history. I had ambition in the world of jurisprudence. Long-winded common sense. What right did my mother have to come and interrupt my rise? How could I pay attention? And what exactly was it she was asking me to consider? That which she could not face herself?

Among my mother's papers I found a card, suitably sombre, which read:

> *Your father died last week. I suppose you will be glad to know. Funeral St. Michael's, 14th Nov, 10:30. Father Fletcher presiding. You would be most welcome.*

She did not go. She hadn't given him much thought when he was alive, so what did it matter now that he was dead?

Now fatherless, Edgar grew. He tried to take over the running of the farm, but he could not plough a straight line, could not shear a clean sheep. His hay bales fell apart in his hands as soon as he lifted them. Season by season the weeds prospered. Under his own volition he would scoot off into the bush. Truant officers never laid an eye on him. Letters came from the bank with increasing frequency, threatening to foreclose, and in time the mother succumbed, selling off the paddocks one by one, which were snapped up by Dungay, their neighbour. He also took the father's cattle dogs, Rex and Bex, off their hands, such a waste to see good work dogs not doing what they were bred for. The mother asked Dungay would he take on Edgar when the hay carting season arrived — but, Dungay lowered his voice, he was afraid that Mrs Dungay did not trust Edgar around their daughters. They were at an impressionable age. Anyone could see that the boy was about to run wild. History repeating itself, eh? The mother was too stunned to answer, and watched Dungay retreat, dragging the father's dogs.

Sometimes the mother, rocking back on a kitchen chair, would make noises which sounded to Edgar like:

'MygodwhathaveIdone?'

Edgar stared at her with his head turned on one side, a chop bone poised in his fingers.

Sometimes it seemed that the father was still alive, clanging about in the shed. Sometimes it felt that the sun stopped still in the sky, or else refused to rise, smouldering below the horizon. Other times he woke and was surprised that months, or years had passed. One morning he stepped into the bathroom and found sprouts of pale hair growing in copses on his face. But not on the pink weal where his lip was sundered like an old feather. He could not remember if they had been there the day before or not.

What he did remember was one day coming down from the edges of the dish that were not hills, a stone in his mouth, his body satisfied like a dog after vigorous exercise. No smoke coming from the chimney. The chickens still not released. The mother's silky burst through the door's torn flywire when it heard him approaching. It barked in frantic orbit about his legs. Inside he found her lying on the floor of the bathroom, beneath the thin fabric of her dressing gown and the chill of the autumn air.

Edgar bundled her up in his arms like a bag of kindling and carried her out to the father's old ute. He had done enough paddock-bashing in it to know roughly what to do. The mother slumped against the door. The ute bounced over potholes and obsolete cattle grids. When he braked too suddenly in a spray of stones at the main road, she slumped forward onto the floor. Edgar jumped out and ran to rearrange her on the seat again, pulling the gown over the pale, doughy flesh he did not wish to see. He wrapped the seat belt around her this time. Her head lolled. The tongue in her mouth large and purple. She moaned: '*Nnn.*'

Edgar apologised continually in the language only she and he understood, telling her to hang on, give it a rub, old girl. He was helping her. Behind them, in the tray of the ute, the silky yapped through the glass of the rear window — the same vantage from which Edgar had often watched the father wrestle the ute into town.

He sped along the highway in third, despite the fear he felt at the open road with the trucks barrelling past. The less complicated gear-changing the better. His hands knew when to turn the wheel. He knew which hairpin corners to navigate carefully — the S-bends at Kapooka, the T-intersection at the golf club. He put the indicator on. He understood the reasons why. The surprise and power he felt at this knowledge fizzed through him. He was driving to the rescue.

He knew the tall red-bricked building, where the highway became Edward Street, was called the hospital. He'd been born here, with the cord around his neck, they'd never tired of telling him. He shouldn't have lived. He sped through the red-lit intersection at Docker Street without stopping.

Horns blared. Tyres screeched. He lurched the ute off the road, through the gate, too fast up the ramp and, as gently as he ultimately could ('Hang orn, Ma'), smashed through the sliding glass doors that formed the entrance to Casualty. The engine stalled. Glass skittered across the polished linoleum. A row of astonished faces all turned towards him. Edgar barely noticed (as his head shot forward and his jaw hit the steering wheel) that his four lower teeth also disappeared amongst the carnage. People ran everywhere, shouting, some of them on crutches. Nurses and other staff came and gawped. Patients sat in hardbacked chairs, bandaged, eyepatched, silent or screaming, staring in shock at the ute and the bloodied driver throwing open the door. The silky in the back yapped without pause. Edgar fell from the cabin and raced around the front of the car. When he released her from the seat belt, the mother fell into his arms. He lifted her from the cabin and stood in the shattered foyer, the mother loose in his arms, her gown gaping. Finally a nurse came to him and led him to a trolley in a corridor where she helped him lay the mother down on a frighteningly clean sheet. He gulped at the blood in his mouth. Spat out a tooth. No sooner had he laid her down than two hefty fellows in security uniforms pounced on him. They tried to pin him to the floor, but

Edgar was strong for his age and it was only with difficulty that all three of them sat down, in some clumsy embrace, with a bump on the floor. Their arms were entangled, while two orderlies quickly wheeled the trolley away and the mother disappeared behind a white door which swung and swung until it swung no more.

When they creaked open the lock-up the copper asked how long had he been driving around with his mother's body in the car? Behind him stood another man in a suit who said he was from the Base Hospital. They stared at Edgar's ravaged face. Edgar did not try to cover it. His bottom lip was split and purple as a slug. His tongue explored continually the space where his teeth had been. He could not grunt his name. He stared at the buttons on the man's suit. Where did such buttons come from?

They took pains to explain that before an autopsy established the cause of death they could only hazard a guess, but until that time his mother would be registered as dead on arrival. It had not been as a result of the impact with the hospital doors.

'But she groaned. She were alive,' said Edgar.

There was a short pause in the conversation. They conferred. While they sympathised with his sudden loss, there was the question of the cost of repairs to the sliding doors. Edgar said nothing. While they understood there was no appropriate time to raise these matters and no delicate way in which to do it, they further understood that there was no insurance cover attached to the vehicle involved in the accident. In addition it was not registered. Nor did Edgar have a licence. This was a delicate situation, they understood, but one that could not retrospectively be overlooked by hospital bureaucracy.

'What about me dorg?'

'Pardon?'

'Me dorg. The silky.'

The two men looked at each other, then at Edgar. Was it the toothlessness or the cleft palate that made him so difficult to understand?

'Do you know what we're talking about?'

Edgar did not. Only that the mother had vanished behind some swinging doors, the silky was missing, and his teeth were also gone.

The policeman made several phone calls while Edgar stood waiting by the desk. The man in the suit went, with perfunctory words of condolence, deep sympathy, terrible tragedy, yap yap yap. They would be in contact regarding the funerary arrangements and that *other matter*, though he did not say who *they* were, or how they would contact him. They wanted the names and numbers of other members of the family so that they could be contacted.

Eh?

The policeman told him that the ute had been impounded. He could not have it back, and without a licence he ought to have had more sense than to drive it in the first place. Didn't he think to phone for an ambulance?

What with?

Edgar made a squiggle on the release papers.

The door. The steps.

The driver of the patrol car stared at him in the rear-view mirror.

'What happened to your face, mate?'

Edgar turned the face to the window. Houses rushing past. Fences. Sprinklers waving their fronds of water on desperate lawns. Kids riding on bikes and skateboards. The life of the town carrying happily on. At the council pound the policeman left him. Edgar found his way up the wooden stairs into the office. A bell tinkled above the door. A large poster of a miserable looking puppy hung on the wall, some vaccination program, Edgar didn't bother with the small print. A girl behind the desk looked up. It was Ivy Cornish. She blinked when she saw him. He also. She no longer wore plaits, but jeans and a chequered shirt. Her hair was shorter. He saw that she still chewed her nails. She asked politely what he wanted.

'Me dorg.'

He breathed deeply. He wanted to tell her about the mother, but did not have the words. He saw that Ivy had chosen not to remember him.

He watched her take a bunch of keys from a drawer, then she led him quickly through to the cages. Past a row of wire pens full of cats. Ivy took a pair of yellow plugs and inserted one in each ear. A man in wet gumboots was hosing down the concourse. The silky set up an immediate high-pitched yapping as soon as it saw him. Other dogs joined in, leaping at the wire, and soon there was a howling, barking cacophony that came to Edgar's ears as a keening wail of grief. He stared at them all behind the wire as Ivy retrieved the silky from its cage. The dog writhed frantically in Edgar's arms. He let it lick his face. Ivy looked away. She would not meet Edgar's eye. They would not chat about school, about the good old days. She was disowning him too. Part of him felt hot with fury. He wanted to bite her fingers off. Part of him was hardening and cracking with sadness. He followed her back to the office, where she marched behind the fortress of her desk, tossed the ear plugs in a bin.

'The old girl kicked the bucket,' he said, lamely.

'That's no good. When?'

'Yesterday.'

'Oh,' she said.

There were some forms for him to sign, the matter of a fee. Edgar saw all the paperwork in that office. He walked straight past her, out into the sunshine. The door. The steps. If she spoke to him he might burst. She pursued him to the doormat, excusing herself! excusing herself! She called out to him from the top of the wooden verandah, her voice strident, 'Sir, sir.' Had she forgotten his name?

Edgar kept walking, the little dog in his arms. Perhaps it wasn't her, perhaps it was her friend —

'Come back here.'

— who had been kind to him. What was her name? Sophie, yes.

'Come back, you —'

He did not turn. Did not hear. His mouth throbbing with every step, down the gravel pathway to the road.

They walked. He had no idea where the ute had been taken. When the silky grew tired he carried her. Beyond the last fibro houses of town where no sprinklers flung their feathers of spray. Maybe Ivy lived in one of them? There were no lawns. The paddocks, stained purple, began to spread towards the horizon. Without the domesticity of fences getting in the way the earth seemed to sigh and stretch, finding its level, luxuriating in its own sweet dust. Their footsteps found a rhythm. Cars occasionally honked, irritated at having to drift around them. They passed the dry, brown fairways of the golf course. Open spaces. Sheep crowded together in the shade of solitary trees, so still they might have been photographs of sheep. Rounding the Kapooka bends, over the rise, the blue silhouette of the Rock again came into view. He lifted the dog over the fence and climbed between the strands of wire, deciding to travel cross-country. Bugger the road. He walked through a rustling stubble of canola — *rape*, as his father called it — in the general direction of the Rock. It wasn't just a barren paddock. Edgar understood, even if he wasn't good at it, the plain hard work that went into persuading it through its seasons.

It should only have taken a few hours to walk the distance by road, but he was forced to detour around several farmhouses and farmers out in their paddocks, who appeared between him and the distant landmark. Sometimes the dogs in these houses set up their warning chorus. He had to stop to dig grass seeds out of the silky's ears when they arrowed their way through her fur. Once the silky rolled in a cow turd, dislodging worms, grinding its muzzle into the golden dung. Edgar did not try to stop it, rather he felt it was a reward after the torment of the pound. It looked like freedom. They walked on, the dog a little prouder in its stink.

The paddocks hummed with insects. Black rags of crows passed overhead. Edgar's feet swished through grass, crunching over stalks of wheat. Cows eyed them warily. Sheep fled. The silky kept by Edgar's side. His anger at Ivy Cornish abated. Mile after mile they walked, clambering through fences. Horses snorted and whinnied at them. The silky yapped, then scampered after Edgar who wasn't afraid of any old horse. Edgar trusted that eventually he would come to a plot of familiar ground. Soon enough he would recognise the hills and dams and dead trees.

At first he identified more general qualities of the landscape other than the distant Rock. The slant of horizon, or a whole copse of trees that had survived the father's manic clearing. A ringbarked redgum with upright branches like a witch's fists clutching at the sky. He walked. Even if he had to traipse the known world, out to the flatlands and back. The slope of a particular incline (they couldn't be called hills); the lean of a particular tree trunk; a creek bed and the contours of its erosions; all began to concur and look familiar. When he knew everything, even the birds in the sky, as the sun was starting to descend, turning the clouds green and purple, he knew he was at this empty place called home.

The house was dark. A few loose weatherboards lay on the ground as if someone had dropped them and run away. No smoke from the chimney. The steps. The door still wide open. Was it only yesterday he had carried the feathery sack of the mother through it? Her chair on the porch. Her box of flour on the kitchen bench. His footsteps echoed. He tapped the water tank by the back door. It gave a hollow clang down to the lowest corrugations. He lit the fire and warmed some food from a tin over the stove and fed half to the dog, adjusting his own chewing in accordance with the changes demanded by his mouth. There had been no electricity since before the father had shot himself that calm afternoon, so he lit a fire in the lounge room too, the owl-eyes of a couple of plough disks deflecting heat out into the room. He patted out several sparks that leapt from the grille. He wondered where was the gun now? He went into the mother's bedroom and stared at the unmade bed. There was hair in her brush on the dressing table. Her wardrobe. It was painful to look at, so he closed the door on those raw frailties, fixing them in his mind. He dragged the blankets off his own bed, the cushions off the couch and slowly fell asleep in front of the dancing characters of the flames. ('Now now, Eddy, I hope yer not dirtyin' them blankets?') It was his place now. No mother to tell him when to go to bed, wash his ears, change his underpants. He could do as he wished.

A rat ran across him in the night. He woke with a start. He slept. He woke, comforted by the certainty that the mother was asleep in the next room. Darkness lasted a long time.

The next day a copper arrived to give him some instructions for the funeral. The swelling in his bottom lip had gone down, and the raw vacancy in his mouth felt less tender, although his tongue was still drawn to it. Was it the same policeman, or another? Edgar could not tell. He was trying to remember how the father had taught him to deal with coppers. Where was the spanner? The silky bared its little pointy teeth. The man read from a letter in his hands: the mother had died of coronary occlusion compounded by cirrhosis of the liver. It was all neatly typed on the sheet of paper he handed over. Edgar crushed it into his pocket. He asked if he would be able to dig the grave himself. The policeman told him if he did that then the Miscellaneous Workers Union, who represented the gravediggers, would blackban his mother's plot and not maintain it. Edgar shrugged — was that a reason why he couldn't dig the hole? The cop shrugged.

'I see you got your dog back.'

'She a good dorg,' said Edgar.

'Pardon?'

'A good dorg.'

'Right.'

Edgar stared at his injuries in the mirror. His swellings would heal. In a way they distracted attention from the anomalous sneer of his top lip, covered with a sparse brown fuzz. His gum was pink and soft, but if he was anything like the father then he'd soon be able to chew on it. If he stuck his jaw out, the canine teeth on either side gave him a look he rather liked, a proper good set of fangs.

A woman approached him at the graveside.

There were a few other people there. A couple of pallbearers, the backhoe operator. Father Fletcher with the whiskers carefully excised from his dimpled chin, his soothing voice struggling against the wind. God may have been invoked. Spits of rain. Edgar made no sense of it. Dungay, the neighbour, was there, in a too-tight suit. The coffin bumped against the clay sides of the hole as the assistants lowered it down. It was a good-looking hole. A neat pile of dirt covered in a tarpaulin. He could have done as good a job. Edgar held the silky in his arms. It kept licking his hand and licking his hand. He wondered did gravediggers ever find any gold? One of the assistants offered Edgar a sprig of wattle, then, when Edgar did nothing with it, motioned for him to throw it into the grave. Dungay and the strange woman did the same.

Dungay shook Edgar by the licked hand. Soothing words. It seemed he was not permitted to watch the backhoe refill the hole. He would have been interested in that. The woman removed her dark glasses and came over to him. She was a fair bit older than Edgar. With wavy hair. She smelled faintly of musk and sweat. Her coat was wet.

'Hello, Edgar,' she said, holding out her hand. It was cold and thin. 'Paul Cornish wrote to me. My name is Lynne. I'm your sister.'

This was the first time I had ever laid eyes on my uncle. I was nearly ten and horrified to think I could be related to this mutant.

'And this is Tony, your nephew.'

He could have been a big-boned teenager, or he could have been fifty, it was impossible for me to tell. Broad across the shoulders, a bush of wiry brown hair alive on his head. I did not want to shake his hand, but she made me do it. Imagine what my friends would have said if they could see me.

Mum had told me about her brother only days before. Why did we have to sit in a car for six hours and drive to this desolate hole in the middle of nowhere for the funeral of some old bag I had never met? Because Mum was going to bury her ghosts. Why couldn't Dad come? Because he refused. If they weren't important enough to visit in life, then it was too late now. Mum hadn't seen her brother since he was a baby.

Her brother! He belonged in a circus. When he spoke his face was a hatchet job of gums and yellow teeth. He spoke like a spaz. And when he shook my hand his fingers were wet. Did he have a clue who we were? I don't think so. A musky woman and a kid who looked like most other kids he had seen, not wanting to meet his eye.

When we drove away I sat sullen in the passenger seat staring out the window at the stupid paddocks. They were still as barren and oppressive as my mum remembered. Made for leaving. I did not want to listen when she explained that his appearance, the cleft palate and the harelip, was how I had also been born. There was an hereditary link. I should feel lucky I was so good looking. If that was the case, then I was never going to have kids. She ruffled my hair. I refused to believe that I had once looked like that monkey man. I wished she'd keep her secrets to herself. But if I could not believe it, what must Edgar, left alone at the graveside, have thought of us?

It took me many years to conjure this question, and when the time came, I forgot to ask it.

It was too much to think about. His brain could not think beyond the landscape. After the funeral Edgar left for the hills, and spent several days in the scrub on and around the Rock. The silky went with him. He found the spot where the fox had torn his arm. Not even the bones remained, out here in the open. Sometimes, in the air around them, coming even from the earth, seemed the music of crows. He thought that these were the sounds of desolation, as well as the sounds of home. From other homesteads on the western side of the Rock neighbouring dogs caught wind of them and set up a nightly wail. Edgar and the silky responded as a duet, howling together in the absence of a moon.

They camped at night on top of the Rock, near the severed throat of the headless lion, with a fire to warm them and random sparks to contribute to the heavens. The faint glow of lights from Henty and Culcairn to the south. At dawn they woke among the stones with frost on their blankets. During the day they never tired of wandering over the gradual waves of hills. The way they rippled towards the eastern horizon or the flatlands to the west. It was an ocean swell that had set like a pudding. They were part of the landscape, like a myth. At the base of the lion's foot they discovered the carcass of a wallaby. It had been pecked clean by ants and crows, leaving the stiffened parchment of its hide. Edgar picked a few wizened gobbets off it, kicked clear the ribs, scoured the skin on a rock. He draped it around his shoulders. It would do for sitting around the fire at night, to keep the wind off, or else for the dog to sleep on. At night the stars prickled the sky and Edgar did not feel alone.

In the cold ashes of the fire Edgar discovered what he thought was a human tooth. He thought this had something to do with the blackfeller business, and left it there.

On the third night, as he gazed into the familiar faces of his fire, the silky commenced a low growl at the darkness all about them. Edgar fed twigs into the flames and watched them burn and contort into coal and ash. He turned potatoes wrapped in tin foil with a stick. In the flickering shadows a pair of red eyes reflected coins of light tossed there by the flames. Edgar studied the eyes, shielding his vision from the fire, until he picked out the shape of a dog sitting, watching them. It might have been a stone in the shape of a dog. He whistled softly. The dog's ears moved. He tossed a few steaming clods of rabbit guts. Rabbit was one of Edgar's favourite foods, especially if he had caught them himself, but not the guts. Ready to flee at any moment, the new dog sniffed apprehensively towards them, one eye on the fire all the time. Its incisor hooked the guts up delicately as a crochet needle. A hot gulp of tongue and they were gone.

By morning he had befriended the new dog. It was a blue heeler bitch, crossed with other bits and pieces. A farm dog, and judging by the dugs on it, fairly due to whelp. It followed them back on the morning's journey to the house along Bullenbrung Road. The hide he had found had cracked and softened already to the contours of his shoulders. He felt like a caveman, insulated against the elements. The bitch would not walk with them, but lagged behind in the gravel. Stopped when they stopped, moved forward when they did. Sniffed at their ablutions.

No smoke from the chimney.

The bitch moved into the laundry. Edgar made a nest for it out of the mother's old rags. There was a blackened scorch mark reaching from floor to ceiling behind a cupboard. The mother had often looked sadly at it. It gave him an idea to burn everything he didn't need in the fireplace or the old combustion stove with the leaky flue. He found a pair of the father's boots in the bottom of the wardrobe and they were a good fit. He practised kicking them off into the corner of the kitchen.

'Pass the salt. Fetch my tea,' he would call out.

'Fetch it yerself,' the mother's ghost replied.

'Do a digger a favour.'

'Bag yer head, yer drongo.'

He amused himself in this dialogue.

Within a fortnight the bitch had given birth to a litter of half a dozen mongrel pups. Edgar watched the labour with interest and let the dog gnaw at his wrist to ease its pain. He was curious to see her eat the afterbirth and lick the clear shit sprayed over the nest by her blind rodents. He watched as they found their way to the teats and latched on. From her position on the floor the bitch stared up at him, helplessly, her eye imparting some message that he could not figure, lying in her rags.

In another week the pups had grown a peach fuzz of fur and were crawling clumsily over each other in the laundry. The silky too observed their progress with interest. Its tail wagged like a metronome. Edgar congratulated the bitch when the pups opened their eyes; gave their first yap; did all the first things that dogs do in their unstoppable urges.

'Good girl, good old girl.'

Survive and grow. Suffer and thrive. Shit and prosper. He began to see the force in this equation.

Edgar ate eggs. He filched them from the secret places chickens hid themselves during the day. He had to watch where they went once he'd released them from their coop. He found one of their favourite hiding places in the tin cathedral of the old shed. The bright invasion of sunlight when he hauled open the door. Its echoing emptiness. The father's old tools were still in there, hung up on old coat hangers, rusting. There were still footprints in the dust on the floor. Bird prints. Mice prints. The dustsquirm of a snake. The peppercorn tree grew over the door, keeping it in perpetual, lacy shade, hot smell of spice in the air. The chickens laid their eggs in boxes of nuts and bolts and nails. When there were no more eggs he began to eat the chickens, plucking then cooking them whole in the firebox. Eating the limbs before feeding the bones, baked gizzards and offal to the dogs.

'Good tucker, eh dorgs?'

The remaining chickens began to look worried.

The pups grew quickly, in direct proportion to the shrinking population of the chickens. Other dogs came to join their pack, including Rex and Bex who made a break from Dungay's chain gang. Edgar welcomed them home and saw they had grown older, greyer. Bex immediately lay down and wanted her stomach scratched. Edgar was pleased they both remembered him. When he had finished his attentions, she lay there, limbs awry in the dust. The leathery studs of her nipples.

Over time he adopted a wayward golden retriever. Also a bull mastiff, a Springer Spaniel, a Staffordshire terrier with half its tail missing, a Great Dane as big as a pony. He admired the way the purebreds could lie flat on their stomachs, hind legs splayed out behind them. Edgar welcomed them all. More the merrier. He enjoyed a sense of freedom he had not imagined when the mother was alive. Mrs Hamilton. When he thought of her, a sense of pale sadness formed in him like a milky ball of dough. It sat in his gut, disrupting his ability to consider anything else. Where was honour and dignity now? During such moments the silky would come and lick his hands. Edgar stroked the soft flesh of its ears, like new leaves. It was the same gesture the father had made with money, but Edgar could not see the similarity. Disliking stillness, the pups would pounce on him, and they would resume their perpetual game of racing up and down the hallway, in and out of rooms, round and round the house. The yard. The surrounding paddocks. Edgar saw great purpose in fostering them. Each week they grew perceptibly bigger and he knew that one of these days he would have to think hard about the implications of this. Or something to that effect.

TWO

Endless exercise.

Dungay watched Edgar and his troop cavort through the lupins and shook his head. From a distance it did not look like he was canine, more that the canines all resembled him. A big strong lad without a father carrying on like a ten-bob watch. Dungay was glad his daughters were safely locked up at nursing school or teachers' college, or wherever they were. That lass who'd gone missing all these years past: too many mysteries there. There were so many dogs he could not tell from a distance whether his own were among them. He suspected they were, but he wasn't about to march over to find out.

Edgar roamed the countryside in every direction, investigating derelict homesteads, not unlike his own, where even the farmers had gone. Houses without roof or wall. Homes for bats and owls. He loved to yank up old sheets of corrugated iron lying about in the grass and chase snakes. They even made their way as far south as the river, defined in the distance by its shadow of trees. Which river was it? He supposed it had a name. Most things did. They drank from it; they swam in it. For Edgar, names were not important. If they followed it far enough to the west they would meet the Murray. If they followed the Murray they would meet the sea. The father had said so.

Edgar recalled comics he had seen. Huckleberry Hound, or Finn, or someone, asleep on a riverbank, fishing. The picture must have come from a book the mother had read to him. Or someone. So he too tied a piece of string about his toe, baited with a piece of parson's nose impaled on a makeshift hook at the other end. He tossed it in and lay back. The sun warm on his face, the orange inside his eyelids. His own snore woke him. Nothing happened except that his toe turned dark and he quickly had to cut the string and rub some circulation back into it. He attempted fishing from different spots along the river, using different toes. He was getting a lot of sleep. Eventually he was wakened by the softest of tugs on his little toe. He hauled in the line, hand over hand, and found he had caught a crayfish refusing to unclasp its claw from the meat. Other times, on different toes he caught yabbies, carp, even a young Murray cod.

After he cooked and ate, he walked. The dogs came at his whistle. If they lost track of the day they would walk at night. Sometimes they gathered together under a tree and slept. Edgar would climb amongst the branches and find eggs. He was a good climber. Cattle fled at their approach, a great tremor rumbling in the ground. Where necessary Edgar restrained the pups with pieces of rope, but the older work dogs knew better than to cause panic in a herd. The pups learned quickly from Rex and Bex, and more often than not they did as he commanded. Edgar found that his brain recalled the father's instructions to the dogs: the whistles and gestures. If one displeased or disobeyed him he would pick it up by the ear and shake it furiously, flinging it away into a tussock of grass, only to have it come fawning back to lick his boots and roll on its back and offer its throat. But he also knew how to reward and favour. He was their master. He was top dog.

Once, in a paddock far from the house, they came across a lame sheep. He did not know whose paddock it was. The beast had been separated from a flock which had fled when the dogs appeared. Too old to keep up. The dogs circled it, manoeuvring it into a corner framed by two intersecting fences. The sheep bleated helplessly at them. With growling threats and imprecations Edgar held the dogs back. A low rumble like the hum of idling machinery came from their throats. They were hungry after their meanderings. The ewe was frozen in terror. Everywhere it turned a dog took a pace forward, the cattle dogs with their hypnotic eye. It bleated again, watching Edgar as he stepped from the pack. Watching as he took the hatchet from his belt, watching as he raised it high and brought it down. Her legs buckled. Knowing it would come to this, Edgar took a step back, and with no more than an attitude, the turn of his body, let the dogs in.

So began, in a modest way, their life of rustling. A heifer or ewe would last the pack several days. After they had eaten their fill out on the plains Edgar would chop up what remained with his hatchet and carry it home in a knapsack. Blood sometimes seeping out of it. He became proficient at slicing up portions for himself with his knife. Edgar-the-butcher. Local farmers blamed feral dogs that lived in the scrubby hills. Bones were found.

Ant-hollowed skulls. Stories returned about a puma descended from ones released by American soldiers after the war. Edgar too had sometimes wondered if the father's stories of the puma were as true as the ones of the beheading of Hanging Rock. Kengol. He had never come across a puma. He would do a Tarzan job on it if he did. In truth, what feral dogs there were, came and joined Edgar's pack. Now he had a Rottweiler, a pitbull, a collie dog, a three-legged Labrador all living happily with him under the one roof, too. Edgar ruled them all. He knew their habits and their predilections. But for a bit of rough and tumble, the dogs, in turn, lavished their love on him. Sometimes he saw Dungay, in his battered hat, come to their common fence and stare across at the house. If Dungay whistled for Rex and Bex, they did not go to him.

One day, resting in the cool of the lounge room, listening to the occasional drone and the snap that silenced a fly, he saw a forest of ears prick up. The low grumbling began in their throats. Hackles rose, then Edgar too was able to hear the sound of the engine approaching.

'Shuddup.'

They waited. He placed aside his empty tin of beans. Through the window he saw a car turn into the yard, heard its slowly turning tyres puff the dust before them. Heard the motor cease. The doors open. A man in a suit stepped from the passenger side. Was it the same suit? The same man? Maybe Edgar needed to get a suit? A woman, similarly dressed, stepped from behind the wheel.

'A woman?' he said to the dogs '— wearin' duds.'

It was as much a mystery to Edgar as it was to the dogs. The two picked their way through the turds in the yard. Disappeared from view. At the far end of the house there was a knock. One of the pups yapped. Edgar punched it. It yelped. Edgar stood. Every dog in the room rose to its feet.

They stood gazing at each other, the stuffing spilling out of the couch, the curtains ravaged. Tufts of dog fur scattered all over the floor. There was another knock. Edgar opened the door into the hall and squeezed through the crack. The dogs tried to slip through with him. He blocked their exit, leaving the barrier of his leg as the last thing he pulled out after him. They whined and scratched at it. One of them gripped his pants leg. They didn't like to be thwarted. He shook his leg vigorously. He dragged the door shut behind him with a soft click. At this small sound there erupted a riot of howling and barking from the muffled confines of the lounge room. Edgar marched down the hallway. He flung open the door to the wide-eyed surprise of his visitors. Visitors. Here on the step. He didn't want to let them in. The house was such-a-mess. The ruckus from the dogs. They stared at him through the shredded flywire, before the woman spoke.

'Mr Hamilton?'

Edgar looked at her lapels, her trousers. She had to make herself heard.

'Mr Hamilton, my name is Kate Shoebridge, I'm from the Department of Community Services —'

She held out her hand and Edgar saw that the colour of her nails — there seemed to be so many of them — looked as though they had been dipped in honey.

'— And here are our cards,' said the man, presenting two identity cards which Edgar did not take. He showed the man his fangs. The dogs in the room behind him were going berserk. The man took a step down from the porch.

'We were simply wondering,' the woman, Kate Shoebridge, continued, 'how you were getting along after the — er, isn't it silly but you can never just come out and say it, you know what I mean, the, er, passing of your mother.'

'Dead as a dodo,' he agreed.

What *was* a dodo?

Edgar listened to the further words of condolence but found it hard to understand. He added a few of his own.

'Me dorgs is hungry.'

'Yes, things must be very difficult. To get to the point, your mother was collecting a pension at the time of her, er, passing. Which included financial support to help with an intellectually disabled son. I guess that must be you, Mr Hamilton.'

'Me dorgs is very hungry.'

He kept looking at her nails. Her duds.

'Let's go, Kate,' said the man, nervously. 'Do this over the phone.'

'What we were curious to know is why you haven't continued to access this support through our office? There is a relatively substantial amount of money, which has not been touched. We wondered if you still continue to require the Department's assistance at all?'

'Whafor?'

'For meeting the daily costs of living, rental, transport, et cetera. We have recently altered our banking arrangements and procedures in order to facilitate —' she looked at Edgar '— in order to make it simpler ... so as to —'

The dogs barked furiously, throwing themselves at the inside walls of the house.

'What can I feed me dorgs? The chooks is all gorn.'

'This keycard will enable you to access a range of different services, for an automatically deducted fee, provided by or in association with the Department.'

Kate Shoebridge flipped open a smart leather wallet and took out an envelope. The man had shuffled down three more steps. There was dog shit everywhere.

'For example,' she was speaking faster now. Edgar came out onto the porch, where they could see his face clearly.

'For example, with this keycard you can set up an account with a number of local businesses that will direct debit your account, plus offer you a pensioner discount on a range of services.'

He took the envelope and brochure that she handed him. 'I've got tea,' he said. They ignored him. He could tell they wanted to leave. They were both at the bottom of the steps.

'You'll have to sign this form as proof of receipt, Mr —'

Before she could say his name they heard the sound of glass breaking from around the corner of the house. The clamour of the dogs was immediately louder. After a rapid glance at one another, Kate Shoebridge and the man both turned and bolted for the car. One of the stupid mongrels had worked itself into such a tizzy it had chucked itself through the damn window. Bugger it! Edgar saw the pitbull charge around the corner. The fleeing ankles. He leaped down the porch steps and ran to intercept it, as Kate Shoebridge and her fancy fellah reached the car. He tackled the dog and rolled over the top of it, tumbling, pinning its head in submission against the earth. One on one was easy. It was the sort of game the dog enjoyed, even when Edgar sat himself on top of it, as the car wheeled a dusty arc around the yard and sped off down the track. Edgar slapped the silly mutt about, then let it pursue the car to the road. He picked up the envelope. He went inside to release the others and smash out the remainder of the window pane before one of them could disembowel itself through mistimed hijinks.

He nailed up his old wallaby hide over the window. It was pretty ragged, but it kept out most of the wind. Whenever he opened the door the draught made the hide slap against the hole in the glass. Like what? He tried to find words to describe it. Like a drunken fuck.

Crows learned to follow them when they set out across the grass on their wanderings. Burrowing through various crops of wheat, barley, canola, Salvation Jane. They were grassdogs. Farmers roved their boundaries at night in paddock-bashers with spotlights mounted on the roof, looking out for sheep duffers, or pumas. Sometimes in the dark silence he heard the snapping echo of rifle shots at the end of a hot day.

It was difficult to find enough to feed them all. The dogs had started to snap at each other in hunger and boredom. The pups, which were nearly full sized, bore the brunt. Edgar had to think of something. There were too many dogs. Somehow he was responsible for them all. He was the provider. It was this vague idea of responsibility which disturbed him. There were over a dozen dogs now. The pups were ravenous. They would eat anything. They ate rabbits blinded by myxomatosis. They ate crows and other birds. They ate old car tyres. They ate cow shit. The fussier silky and the three-legged Labrador grew weaker. Edgar kept tidbits aside for himself and them. They hungered, but they survived.

Eventually, one morning Edgar packed his knapsack with things they would need and headed off for town. It was not really a decision he made, but simply something his legs started doing. Tufts of elephant grass still crisp with frost as they set out, breath foggy from their muzzles. The orange sun through the mist, coated with mould. The dogs raced ahead of him and around him. The silky and the Labrador stayed by his side. No matter how fast he walked they did not lag behind. They strained without question. The burrs and grass seeds stuck to the dogs, matting their fur. When they stopped to rest, Edgar spent time combing his fingers through them, picking them out. The short-haired dogs fared better.

Several other dogs joined them as they journeyed across the winter paddocks towards the big town. The pack was friendly. More the merrier. It took most of two days to walk the distance. However they did not take a direct route, nor did they have anything to hurry for. They were a river of dogs. Loose skeins of cloud drifted high above, floating to the east, foretelling cold nights. The paddocks rolled smoothly beneath his feet, they could not be called flat. Not flat like the flatness further west, out past Lockhart and Urana to Hay where the father had taken him in the ute. Out to Conargo and the Hay plain, to the flat earth. Out there the father had said it was so flat you could feel the holes in your shoes. A limp made you walk in circles. The people there wore ironing boards for hats. The horizon's shadow shimmered. The flatness was oppressive to those who were not used to it. It did not have the same smells he knew. Edgar did not head in that direction. When the landscape undulated, as it did around here, he knew he was in what the father called his own sweet hole.

They travelled overland, crossing the Olympic Way unseen, as if to intersect with the course of the sun. They sniffed out and lapped the water in shallow, brown dams. Once they startled half a dozen mallards, which flapped into the air, dripping pearls of water, each catching a scratch of sunlight. The air was filled with the rushing of wind over their wings, as he and the dogs stared upward. Edgar watched them out of sight, quacking nasally, seeing in his mind's eye the silver drips fall from the sun. They rested against the windbreaks of fallen trees. They slept in the lee of a half-built haystack. Left the next day at dawn before its builder returned. While he was daunted by the demands of his responsibilities, Edgar loved this companionable, aimless end. He wished it might never finish. When they reached Ladysmith, Edgar knew they had walked too far. No matter, there was no hurry. They turned north-west, to the guttering sun, and back towards the big town. They slept. Three other dogs joined them: a frightened Doberman, a moulting Afghan, a one-eyed mongrel. Edgar lashed them with rope as they walked, so they would learn that he was the centre of their meandering orbit. The others ran ahead investigating clumps of bracken, snuffling down old rabbit holes. Their barking resounded off the sides of hills, echoing out of gullies. They frightened rabbits out of grassclumps. But when he whistled, they always returned to his side, like a disparate swarm of bees.

The name of the big town was Wagga. The crow town. It was a town of suburbs and knee-high fences. It was also a town of hospitals and schools and churches and death. The silky yapping in the broken glass on the linoleum floor, the white door swinging to stillness. At his feet the old silky kept pace, despite its greying fur, one ear turned inside out, tongue lolling towards the ground.

They moved as one down the main arterial highway. Crossed Kyeamba Creek and circled behind the RAAF base at Forest Hill. Edgar leashed each dog with the pieces of rope he carried in his knapsack. He tied the rope ends together so that they pulled against each other. Together they hauled him along at a brisk trot. He had to dig his heels in.

'Woah, Dobbin,' he cried in the mother's voice.

To stop them he simply sat down, issuing imprecations. He was the fulcrum. Coming back to the highway they passed yards full of bulldozers, front-end loaders; truck rental companies and the stoneworks. Apart from the traffic, they met an increasing number of bemused pedestrians. They crossed Lake Albert Road towards the central shopping precinct of the city. Kerb and guttering. On Baylis Street they caused a minor traffic jam as they negotiated the crossing of the road. People stared. Shopkeepers came out of their doorways to watch them pass. Delivery drivers let jaws gape at the spectacle of one man with the mottled hotch-potch of dogs passing up the main drag.

It was not difficult for Edgar to find a supermarket. He remembered waiting in the back of the ute while the parents went into one. Merely had to follow the traffic. There, ahead, he saw the massive car park. Then he followed the shoppers, who scurried before him, herded through the automatic doors. A shower of hot air fell on him as he passed through. Why? Inside Edgar stood by one of the cash registers. The dogs tangled around his legs. He blinked at the fluorescent light; the hum of commerce. The hairs on his arms sensed electricity. A girl behind the nearest till stared at him, fingers poised in the act of tapping at the keys. He could not name the look on her face, only that it was a familiar one. Same with the tidy queue of patrons.

'Youcan'tbringthoseanimalsinhere,' she shrieked.

Edgar didn't hear. He stood there with the twenty (or was it more?) leashes gripped in his hands. The silence spread. The pinging tills fell silent, their batteries running. Soon every person in sight, employee and customer alike, was staring at Edgar.

'Isayyoucan'tbringthoseanimalsinhere.'

Edgar raised the bouquet of rope ends he held in his fists.

The public address system crackled and announced:

'Mr Ashcroft, please report to register fourteen. Mr Ashcroft, please come to the front immediately.'

Edgar waited. He liked waiting. Someone laughed. A shopping trolley clashed against another. The dogs were very obedient, even the mongrel pups, as if sensing their moment in the limelight, though some of them had their tails between their legs. They raised their snouts to all the wondrous smells inside the store. Edgar could smell chickens roasting in a rotisserie somewhere in the building's depths. After a while a round man in a suit came bustling along an aisle towards the tills. Where did all these men in suits come from? The round man's jaw dropped when he saw all the dogs. Edgar could see his tongue. He had been eating liquorice.

'What on earth? You can't bring those — What do you mean by? — Those animals are unhyge —'

'Me dorgs is hungry.'

'I don't care what they are, you can't bring them in here — Get them —'

'Me dorgs is hungry.'

Again Edgar held up the rope ends to show Mr Ashcroft. One or two of the dogs strained against Edgar's grip. The click of their claws snickered against the polished floor. Taking a hasty step backwards, Mr Ashcroft held up his hands and squeaked:

'All right, all right.'

He turned to two of the packers who had stopped stacking shelves to watch the spectacle.

'Go and fetch some dog food.'

The two young lads jumped into action, before one of them stopped:

'How many?'

'I don't know. Fill a trolley. Quick smart.'

'And a chook,' said Edgar.

'And a chicken,' Mr Ashcroft called out. Then turning to Edgar, 'It's coming, it's coming. Please don't let them loose.' Then turning to his staff, 'Get back to work, you lot.'

One by one the registers began to ping.

When the trolley was brought to Edgar, replete with assorted cans of dog food of no particular brand, and a chicken wrapped in an alfoil bag, he tried to hand the keycard Kate Shoebridge had given him to Mr Ashcroft. Mr Ashcroft waved him away, casting terrified glances at the dogs.

'Go, just go.'

He ushered Edgar and the dogs beyond the perimeter of the sliding doors. Edgar wheeled the trolley out into the sunshine. The dogs, sensing they had accomplished some common goal, hauled Edgar and the trolley up the footpath, feeling entirely happy with their morning's work, and the unexpected kindness of men in suits.

He hacked open the cans with his hatchet. The dogs scoffed the contents behind some canna lilies in a park. Everyone ate their fill. There were still a few tins left for later. He packed them into his knapsack, left the trolley behind the bushes. Thought it better not to draw attention to himself by wheeling it through the streets. After all, it was not his.

They headed north out of town, crossing the rickety bridge over the flowing current of the mighty Murrumbidgee River — *that sucking mama*: he thought that was what the father had called it. Edgar loved the river. He had fished in it, slept on its banks, bathed and played in it. Somewhere along the way today they had picked up another dog, a boxer. Edgar liked the boxer. He felt some affinity with its squashed, repugnant face. Where possible they avoided busy roads, crossing fallow paddocks without sign of industry. There were more of those in recent times. In the long grass the dogs were hidden from view. Wind caught the top of the grass, washing currents through it. They moved like fish, scattering smaller fry ahead of them.

Edgar's attention was caught by a derelict shearing shed sitting in long, neglected weeds. A row of wildly swaying sugar gums lined the rotten fences around it. Wind muscling its way across the plains. The sorting pens rotting. So, too, some of the stumps. Edgar tested the steps up to a wooden door which, with the help of a hip, creaked open. Within the dimness the wings of an alarmed owl rowed overhead, its silhouette disappearing through a hole in the roof cavity, as easy as you like. The dogs whined with pleasure at the rich smells within, the polished woodwork of the railings worn smooth and dark with lanolin. The previous occupants had departed so suddenly that they had left whole fleeces in the stalls. Unfinished bales lay all over the place. The electricity was still connected. He tested the lights, then switched them off. He had lived so long without electricity, no point in starting now. The dogs sniffed orgiastically amongst the tufts of wool and old droppings. There was enough in the loose bales to make a bed for everyone. Protected from the elements. Shelter. The bustling wind swept up under the wide slats between the floorboards. The rafters were alive with a traffic of rats. The dogs twitched in their sleep. The tin walls and tin roof ticked throughout the night.

When the storm struck, thunder rolling across the sky, some of the pups came to him whimpering for protection. They buried their heads under his legs, in his armpits, at each crack of thunder. He sat there and comforted them as best he could, thinking about all that he had.

Of course in the deceptive heat of the early morning sun, the corrugated iron heated up quickly, ticking now like crickets. There were no windows. Already humid, Edgar imagined what it might be like in summer as they went outside and rested in the shade beneath the shed. The long-haired dogs pulled skeins of wool from their fur, like wisps of cloud. Edgar found an old handset of rusty clippers and trimmed the mangy tufts of hair on the Afghan. He clipped the hair out of the eyes of the spaniel. Edgar-the-gun-shearer. In the evening when the grass turned the colour of rum the dogs chased down a young kangaroo. By the time Edgar had caught up with the pack there was little left of it. Cartilage and bone. Every tail wagging. He divided what gobbets remained to make sure that the smaller dogs got some, and the three-legged Labrador, which he called Tripod, because the old father had once described for him a drover's dog . . . it was too rude to repeat. When the sun went down, the evening cooled quickly. Edgar knocked a few possums from the rafters overhead, but by morning there was no more food, and the dogs were hungry again. That was the trouble with dogs.

They spent several days foundering in this fashion before they made their way back to town and to the supermarket. Not quite a conscious decision, more an instinct. Like moose, or birds migrating. All sorts of rubbish was caught in the tangle of roots along the riverbank. Anything might be hidden there, he thought. The treasures of scavenging. They swam across the freezing water, which came from somewhere in the Snowies. Only one of the dogs, a schnauzer, was taken away by the current. It yapped frantically, its head high above the water, as it disappeared like a paddleboat around a bend, hidden by willows. Edgar did not fret. Easy come. And he was right, for as they walked on it caught up with them eventually, wagging its docked stump of a tail.

'Good dorg. Down now.'

He patted its head, and several of the dogs rubbed noses with it. Welcome back, old friend.

* * *

They stood by the cash register, listening to the tinny music from the local radio station. Customers all staring. He liked waiting.

'*Mr Ashcroft, could you come to the front please,*' said the PA system. '*Mr Ashcroft, he's here again.*'

The round man in the suit came to the front, walking slowly, as if in a church. One of the dogs tried to jump up on him. Edgar could not read the expression on his face. Mr Ashcroft snatched Edgar's plastic card — a dog growled — and took it to a cash register, where they did some monkey-business with it. A trolley was filled. His card returned. There was even a chicken he had not asked for. They were so kind.

'Don't come back here again,' said Mr Ashcroft, 'or I'll call the police.'

Edgar took the dogs away. Everyone was happy. They ate at a popular picnic spot by the river. Wagga beach. After their tin-food frenzy they tore up and down the bank which was now eroding, washing downstream in the current. They splashed in and out of the cold water.

Innocent anglers, kayakers, people out for a stroll, were forced to walk briskly away, terrorised by the dogs which took anarchic control of the beach.

Dogs barked at everyone. On the far side of the river, horses gazed anxiously with ears erect at all this activity, their reflections distorted in the steadily moving water. The dogs barked at them playfully. A car pulled into the car park, which the dogs surrounded. When no one emerged to satisfy their curiosity, they ran off. Edgar fancied he saw someone pointing either binoculars or a camera at him through the sun-bright refractions of the windscreen. What did he care? It was a public space. Once they had eaten and washed and swum, Edgar and his pack moved off along the river, following a well-worn track along the levee bank, through the twisted willows.

Over the following weeks and months Edgar discovered there were seven or eight supermarkets in the greater metropolitan region of Wagga. The staff — all of them cooperative and generous. Their managers, men in suits all, though some with their coats off and sleeves rolled up, studied him with shocked, fishy looks on their faces. The inland town had much to pride itself on, apart from being the biggest inland town. Edgar could see why. It was this universal spirit of cooperation and altruism. They gave him all he wanted. Usually he just stood there. They would take his card and shunt him away with trolleys piled high with tins of dog food. So friendly. Most of the time. Only once, when someone swore at him and threatened to call the police, did he have to release the rope of one of his dogs, or was it an accident? A German short-haired pointer, which bounded off the length of an aisle, barking at its momentary freedom, skidded on the lino, then bounded back. It was as if a puma had been released in the store. People screamed. They must have thought the whole rabid pack was about to be loosed.

Once he arrived to find a police car sitting out the front. Something must be going on, he thought, so, given his memories of police, he went elsewhere. Spreading his visits between the seven or eight supermarkets, Edgar was able to keep all his dogs (he'd lost count of them now) well fed and happy. He never failed to be thankful for the generosity of men in suits who managed the supermarkets. And they never failed to take advantage of his card. He did not want for anything. If he felt like a bag of oranges, or a sack of spuds, or anything else, for that matter, they would give it to him, even if they did seem a bit grumpy. It was never short of amazing, the things he found in tins.

One day he was stopped by the police while pushing his trolley towards the river. It was the copper who had taken him to the council pound to fetch the silky when the mother had snuffed it. The staffy snarled and the policeman drew his gun. Edgar stepped in front of the dog.

'They's all my dorgs,' he said.

'Where did you get the food, Ed? You got a receipt for all this?'

How did he remember Edgar's name? Edgar nodded in the direction of the supermarket.

'Just move over there a bit.'

Edgar hauled the dogs away from the trolley. The cop rummaged through it and found a receipt for purchase. He told Edgar the law required him to keep his dogs leashed at all times. Edgar showed his rope ends.

'Well, you've got to keep 'em off the streets. If one of them bites someone — I dunno — Ed, we've got our eye on you.'

'I ain't done nothing wrong.'

'If I see them in town again I'll impound them. I don't know how you can afford to keep feeding them.'

'You want me ter let 'em go?'

The policeman shrugged and drove away, followed by a woof from the silky.

Keep 'em off the streets, eh? So Edgar took them to a nearby park to feed, where a family of picnickers was forced to flee.

* * *

The Afghan's coat grew thick and glossy, though with occasional bald patches, if one cared to search. Sometimes they slept in one or other of the various parks about the city. Or in the showgrounds. Or in the abandoned shed which they had made their own. Their hidey-hole. Or, when the weather grew warmer, along the riverbank behind the windbreak of the levee. This need for shelter was satisfied by various means so that they did not have to think about it. By and large they lived moment by moment. Usually they were left in peace. Sometimes, marching across vast paddocks, to keep the flies out of his mouth, Edgar tied an old handkerchief over his face. Sometimes he thought of returning to the parents' farmhouse, but the hike was too far. No supermarkets down that way. They would have to come back straightaway for food.

One day as they returned over the grass-covered camber of the hills towards the shearing shed, the lead dog, Rex, stopped in his tracks and flared his hackles. One by one the others followed suit. Creeping through the grass they burst into their shed and in an instant the dogs had cornered a bedraggled-looking man in one of the stalls. The stranger cowered beneath an old fleece, bleeding from the scratches he caused himself in cowering.

'Call 'em off, call 'em off. I give up,' the man cried.

Edgar, hatchet in hand, appeared behind them and called the dogs off.

'They ain't dangerous.'

The man lowered his hands and examined Edgar. Edgar saw that two of the man's fingers were missing.

'You aren't a cop.' The man removed his hat and twirled it in his hands.

'Nope.'

'These aren't police dogs?'

Edgar gestured to the three-legged Labrador, the silky, the spaniel, the schnauzer.

'Nope.'

'Thank Christ for that. I hate those dogs.'

The man calmed down. He sponged some blood off his thumb with a tuft of wool.

Seeing he was harmless, Edgar fed the remaining tins from his knapsack to the dogs. The man watched Edgar at his work, chopping the tins apart, then scooping the contents out into some plough disks he had found.

'Are these all your dogs?'

Edgar ignored him. Feeling safer, the man came out of his stall.

'Mate, are these all your dogs?'

Edgar nodded.

'Haven't you got a can opener?'

'I got a axe,' said Edgar, wiping the blade of the hatchet clean, then licking his finger.

'Isn't there a law against owning so many dogs?'

'Dorgs is dorgs. They foller me. Nobody wants 'em.'

'How do you know nobody wants them?'

''Cause they here. They's grass dorgs.'

'What's your name, mate?'

'Me name?' said Edgar. 'Ed.'

'Well, I'm Meacham,' said the man.

They shook hands and Edgar felt the absence of the fingers, like a girl's hand. Meacham retrieved a bottle of rum from beneath his fleece on the floor: 'Have a snort.'

They sat in the open doorway, their legs hanging over the smooth edge of the shed floor.

'I thought you was a cop.'

'I ain't a cop.' Then remembering his father's lesson, 'I'd hit meself on the bloody noggin with a spanner if I was a cop.'

'That's the ticket,' said Meacham. 'Never tell 'em anything.'

'You was about to spill the ketchup when I come in here,' Edgar pointed out.

'That's 'cause I thought you had all these police dogs. I hate those dogs. These dogs are all right.'

The three-legged Labrador sidled up to Edgar, leaning against him. Edgar scratched its breastbone, in the small place where dogs cannot reach. The Labrador gazed, transfixed, into the far-off blindness of its body. With great tenderness Edgar stroked the stump, the blunt shoulder bone beneath the skin.

After a while Meacham asked, 'What happened to your face?'

'What happened to yer fingers?'

'Fair point,' said Meacham. 'Look at us. What a trio: me fingers; your teeth; his poor leg.'

Edgar wondered which was his nose-picking finger.

'We's all missing something,' said Edgar. 'I got a monolith for a head.'

'They can whittle you down but they can't take your fuckin' dignity. Not if you never tell 'em nothing.'

'Who?'

'The jacks, of course.'

'Oh. Did the jacks lop off yer fingers then?'

'Nah, it was a chain saw.'

Meacham sucked his thumb where he had torn it on a nail.

'Don't suppose you've got a Band-Aid?'

'Nope.'

They watched the moon come up over the paddocks stained with dusk. One or two stars appeared. They passed the rum back and forth. Edgar noted its similarity to the colour of the grass. The man, Meacham, after wiping the mouth of the bottle with his sleeve, guzzled long. Ahh. He passed it over. The alcohol burned Edgar's gums. He heard the father in his exhalation. Some of the rum spilled through the scraps of his beard. He felt somehow grown-up, but sensed that this wasn't enough. Crickets clicked in the grass. Single spats of rain like footsteps on the roof. A few of the pups pricked up their ears, or woofed where they lay, but were not curious enough to get up and investigate. Perhaps they could hear distant thunder. There was an array of fleascratching and dicklicking. The sky sat over them like a conjurer's cloak.

'I don't suppose you've got any tucker?'

'I already et.'

'I'm starving.'

'I got a bag of oranges.'

'That'll do.'

It did not strike Edgar to ask why the stranger had come to be in the shearing shed, in a neglected paddock in the middle of — where was it? — nowhere. He was ready to accept Meacham's presence, as the dogs did, listening instead to the sound of the man's words, which were hypnotic and soothing. The sound of his voice sending bubbles up Edgar's spine. The peaceful sedation of company.

As the bottle emptied, and they sucked their orange pith, the man told Edgar how strange he thought it was, the influence the stars and magnetic poles of the earth had on the lives of people. Strange also the influence and repercussions a simple act in one life could have upon the outcome of another. ('D'ya know what I mean, Ed?') Edgar nodded, looking out the door, up at the guilty stars, though he had not an inkling what Meacham was talking about. The guilty stars twinkled. Meacham was a gambler. He had ruined not only his own life but also the lives of all those who were dearest to him. Gambling had destroyed his happiness. If truth be told he would rather gamble than eat. Horses, dogs, pokies, roulette, two-up, blackjack, anything. Two flies up the proverbial wall. He once had a nice house in a nice suburb in Sydney. A nice wife called Aileen. A good job. Aileen had no idea as to the extent of his problem. He spent his wages on card machines in city hotels. He was very protective of the machines he was playing, and if anyone pulled a jackpot out of a machine he had walked away from in disgust, then yes, he would be prepared to do an injury to that person. Not that he ever did, of course, but he knew the price of a broken limb. He bet on horses he did not know the names of. He had stolen money from his employer. He took savings from his children's education account. He knew it was a cliché but he loved his wife more than all the sand on all the shores, even — the family home had been mortgaged and lost — after she had left him. Debt collectors beat him up. He knew that all he had to do was make one big killing and all his problems would be solved. Every debt repaid. His house reclaimed. Family returned. But Aileen would not return. His debtors wanted their money, like yesterday. (He held up his remaining fingers.) They would settle for his appendages. The last thing he had of value in the world was his father's watch. See. Horsham High School, 1932. In desperation he had taken a samurai sword and held up the cashier in a petrol station in Five Dock. He was drunk and knew he should not have done it, but by Christ it was fun, even though he'd only managed to get fourteen hundred dollars. Not much in the face of the stars' malevolence towards him. The cashier had laughed. Refused to open the register. So Meacham had whacked her with the sword. Not the edge of it, which was blunt anyway — he'd been careful to turn it aside so only the flat of it caught her on the upper arm. A tiny scratch, a shaving nick. Silly bitch had screamed the shop down, and Meacham had been forced to hit her with his fist, smack smack smack, until she shut up. She shouldn't have laughed at him. Didn't she realise that armed robbery was a serious business? So it was obvious for all to see, in his case at least, how in the painful trajectories of the stars, people's fates were decided. Chance was rigged. How had he been reduced to this? That woman, for instance, would probably have nightmares, it was true, as a result of the course of his actions. In this way people were like billiard balls, forever clashing and glancing off each other, conspiring to evolve. Think of the others, the hundreds of others whose lives were maybe changed for the better by entering the realm of his influence, and he himself whose course had been altered, for better or worse, by the impact of others in his past.

'Who knows, Ed, maybe one of those people I've come across in my time, maybe one of them might do some good in the world. Decide to become a doctor or something. Help people. No way of knowing how the dominoes might fall. Take tonight, Ed, no one knows what you'll take from our little chat, how that might change your destiny. Or me too. Maybe meeting you is what I need to set me back on the rails. Take stock. Make my peace with Aileen. Maybe not. That's the bloody stars for you.'

There were no stars now. They had been hidden by a sheet of swiftly moving cloud, as the formative storm moved eastward. Clouds to the north lit silently with flashes of far-off lightning.

Where was the sword now? he wanted to know.

'Chucked it in the river,' Meacham said. 'Anything left in that bottle?'

Edgar stepped down off the shed floor into the darkness. Several dogs looked up to see where he was going. The rest slept. He urinated into the grass. Insects hopped over his bare feet. The sound of frogs in a dam, hidden by spinifex. The frogs silenced by the hissing of ducks as they landed in the shallows. The sibilance and whirr as the ducks took off again. He imagined the water falling from their feet. In gaps between clouds they saw that the moon had moved well overhead, a bright ring around it like a cataract in an old dog's eye. The moon-shadows of the animals lounging in the grass.

'Ed,' Meacham called out after him, 'Ed, you won't tell anyone you saw me here, will you?'

Edgar shook his head. He understood. No business of his.

Edgar watched Meacham traipse over the paddocks, heading north towards Junee. Again he urged Edgar to silence. ('You tell people your dreams and they screw you.') He kept his head down and did not deviate from his path beneath the open sky. Not a trace of storm. Was that his true direction? Was he rather not heading the opposite way, towards the river and the township? Was he lying about where he was heading? Edgar could not tell. The grown pups woofed at him once or twice, then when he had receded beyond interest, burrowed beneath the shed. Clouds of dust billowed out with their digging. They were hungry again. They searched the long grass, but there was nothing for them. They looked at Edgar mutely as if expecting him to magically produce a trolley full of food. He could not. He grabbed his knapsack and again they headed towards the town. The dogs, knowing their purpose, slid through the grass like eels, only the head of the Great Dane visible like some submerged sea monster.

They bypassed the small township of Gumly Gumly and entered the precincts of the city along the Sturt Highway. The truck rentals. Warehouses. Cars slowed to observe them, but Edgar had each dog lawfully tethered to a piece of rope. In town they crossed the parklands over Tarcutta Street. A circus had arrived and set up shop in Bolton Park.

'That's one bloody big tent.'

The dogs were beside themselves at the sight of five elephants chained by the ankles, outside the main tent bestrewn with light bulbs. The creatures rocked themselves slowly from side to side, their trunks snuffling the sawdust at their feet. Edgar had never seen an elephant, nor the size of their turds. He stood watching them for a while, hoping one might snap its chains and run amok. Eventually a man marched across the oval and called out to Edgar from a distance (he dared not come too close; there were some mean-looking dogs). He waved his arms and called out:

'Piss off with them dogs, they're spookin' the elephants.'

Edgar tugged on the ropes, and with some difficulty, the pack moved on. Edgar called back:

'Well, yer elephants is spookin' me dorgs.'

The man did not respond. Edgar thought about this exchange. He had never considered before that he possessed anything akin to wit. He kept replaying the phrase over and over in his mind. *Well, yer elephants is spookin' me dorgs, yer drongo, yer useless halfwit*, and other variations.

It was the turn of the big supermarket in the centre of town. The last time he had been here it had been raining and the dogs left muddy paw prints all over the floor. He wondered if Mr Ashcroft was frightened of dogs? Everyone was most generous. No one went hungry as long as he removed the animals from the premises forthwith. It was a happy arrangement. All the other people he saw there must have come to some similar understanding of their own.

As he arrived on the footpath outside the big brick building he heard a voice distinguish itself from the hubbub of the traffic around him.

'Mr Hamilton?'

It was a woman. A small woman. He looked around. Mr who? There was no one else on the footpath.

'Mr Hamilton?'

'Yerp.'

'Mr Hamilton, my name's Kate Shoebridge. We met out at your parents' farm.'

Edgar remembered. Duds. He had her keycard in his flyblown knapsack. With wagging tails the dogs surrounded her. She stood very still, looking distraught as they snuffled at her trousers, but soldiered on.

'I'm so glad I found you here. I have some news, which might be of interest. It's about your parents' property as a matter of fact. Your property, I mean. It's not normally the province of our Department, but you couldn't be found, and we were approached. My fiancé works in real estate, you see. Someone wants to buy it. An offer has been made. Do you have time to come with me and I'll explain the benefits to you and the implications for your pension? It's just around the corner. These dogs, they're not savage, are they?'

Did he have time? Edgar thought about this. She looked as though she was sinking in dogs.

'Not ter me are they savage.'

'Do you think we could disentangle ourselves and walk to my office? I can offer you a cup of coffee.'

She laid a cool hand on his arm. Her fingers were covered in rings. She seemed to have more twinkling fingers than were necessary. Look at the colours she had painted the nails! She was very brave. The dogs watched her every move. They saw she wasn't going to attack him. Edgar expertly tied all the rope ends — was it sixteen or was it more? — to the poles of two street signs. Edgar thought the presence of the dogs outside the door would remind the staff inside the supermarket to fill a trolley for him. Save time. The two groups of animals almost blocked the wide footpath, barking crazily as he walked away from them with Kate Shoebridge. He was strolling up a wide footpath with a woman — not a bad-looking woman, up a footpath, past shops. The morning sun reflecting off the second-storey windows. He was curious about the notion of whether or not he had time. One thing he knew, at that moment he did not have a care in the world. He wondered if she might touch his arm again.

Her office was of an open-plan design, shared with a lot of other people separated by partitions into what looked like kennels. When he came in they suddenly seemed very busy, bustling about with pieces of paper, avoiding his eye. Edgar scratched a flea which gnawed his scalp. He did not understand the language Kate Shoebridge was speaking to him, but it appeared that one of the neighbouring farmers (Dungay) wanted to buy up his parents' house and the few remaining acres. He understood that much. Then came ... *the financial remuneration of such a sale which would inevitably have an effect, as a result of the mandatory means test, on the level of his welfare support*. Whew. Incidentally, was Edgar receiving any other form of income support and not declaring it? Nup. Did he still have the keycard she had given him? Yep. He patted his knapsack. Why hadn't he read his correspondence? Can't read.

Did he take sugar? Yep. How many? Four. Edgar raised the coffee cup awkwardly to his mouth. Kate looked away. The coffee burnt his tongue. She passed him a tissue. He ate twelve biscuits. He was given a sheaf of papers to consider, plus the business cards of a number of real estate agents, her fiancé's she particularly recommended. She did not offer to consider them for him. Of course he did not have to make a decision now, just to think about it.

One thing that filled Edgar with dread was the prospect of choice. Couldn't he just leave thinking about all this until later? Dungay already had a house. It wasn't as though he and his bloody daughters were homeless. He put the cup down, stuffed the papers into his bag, her tissue in his pocket. She gave the bag a horrified glance. They shook hands and he felt all the thin bones of her fingers. He left the office feeling less at ease than when he had entered. A bank of grey cloud had hidden the sun, in the same way that a neighbouring farm could swallow another.

He trudged purposefully back to the supermarket. When he turned the corner into Baylis Street, he saw from a distance, with a jolt to his heart, that all the dogs were gone. A police car was parked on the footpath. He ripped the tissue from his pocket and threw it on the ground. Even the rope ends were gone. Through the glass doors, as he drew nearer, a plump Mr Ashcroft was talking to the jacks, who had their notebooks open, writing something, or perhaps they were drawing his picture?

Edgar spent a lonely night back at the shed. Every noise louder than before. No dogs returned. The next morning he marched south across paddocks in fury and grief at their loss. And in as much determination. He was convinced Kate Shoebridge was behind it, with her smooth words and cool hands. He kicked the grass apart as he moved through it. Ploughing had begun down this way, and Edgar marched brazenly across the rippled corrugations which had the same texture and pattern as the roof of a dog's mouth. Great clods of dirt fell out of his way. He did not care who saw him. In his head he was hatching a plot.

By the afternoon his mood calmed when, broaching a rise near the backroads behind Uranquinty, he looked up and saw the familiar blue sphinx of the Rock. When he reached the house, for he did not really think of it as a home (no smoke from the chimney), he discovered a number of calling cards shoved under the door. He hadn't locked it. It had never been locked. Every time he came back here it felt emptier. The wallaby hide had fallen off the gaping hole of the lounge-room window. Dust and gum leaves had blown in. Where had the leaves come from? There were no trees within sight, apart from the old peppercorn over the shed. Purple thistles of Salvation Jane had crept right up to the walls of the house. There was bird cack on the kitchen table. When he opened the door of the combustion stove a mouse jumped out and skittered across the floor. Mudwasps had built nests in the corners of the ceiling. When he broke one open with a stick the numbed bodies of small spiders fell to the floor, their legs moving slowly in the air.

In the shed Edgar found all that he needed to fulfil his cunning plan. He shoved everything into the knapsack along with the calling cards, the hatchet, his knife. That night he lay on his old single bed. The emptiness of the building without the dogs or the mother was oppressive. He thought of her dresses falling apart inside their wardrobe. The slap on the roof of a loose piece of tin. He heard the ants at work in the wood. Herds of rats rumbled in the ceiling, grinding their teeth against the beams in the wall behind his head. The step of the mother in every creaking floorboard.

In this loneliness even his fleas were a comfort.

At dawn, shivering, he broke apart a wooden chair and made a fire in the Bega stove. There were still tins of food in the pantry, behind a veil of spider web. He cooked in relative comfort, sitting before the open door of the stove, feeding twigs and other bits of rubbish into the flames. Real estate business cards and brochures. The emptiness he felt was not hunger, though he forced himself to eat. He did not ask himself what he ought to be doing now, he was doing it.

In a while he heard an engine rumbling up the twin channels of the driveway. Edgar stepped out onto the porch, still chewing. The old ute stopped and a man unfolded himself from the seat belt.

'Ed, I didn't realise you'd come back.'

It was his neighbour, Dungay, dressed in a bib-and-brace. Edgar looked at the vehicle. Was it the father's ute? He could not tell.

'I saw your smoke, Ed. Been keeping an eye on the place for you. Thought it might've been —' but what he thought it might have been he did not elaborate. 'There was some woman came looking for you. A gov'ment woman.'

Edgar nodded. Dungay's eyes were shaded under the brim of a large hat.

'I told her you'd gone. Didn't know where. The sister's maybe. I guess you'll be fixin' the joint up again. Like your old dad had it running, eh? Like greased clockwork, ha ha. Needs a lick of paint but. The old girl'll come up nicely in a new skirt.'

He looked up at the sky.

'Arse has fallen out of the wheat market.'

Edgar looked at him. Dignity in silence.

'Me dogs ran off, Ed. The ones your old mum sold me. You haven't seen 'em, have you? Good dogs they was. Trix and Bix. Paid good money for 'em. Maybe the dog-catcher caught 'em? Well Ed, better be going. Machinery to fix. Good to see you. Catch up some time.'

Dungay fell back into the ute and flicked a finger in goodbye.

Edgar shouldered his knapsack and headed out later that morning. There was no hurry. He had all the time under the sun. He liked the metallic rattling noise he made as he walked. Like the couplings of a train moving slowly past the wheat silos at Yerong Creek. He kept thinking about Dungay's hat. That was sensible. Edgar should get himself a hat like that, but Edgar wasn't sensible. He followed the railway line and, for amusement, threw rail ballast at crows. Sheep crowded together in the doomed shade of single sugar gums. No train came. The various dams he saw were drying up, with margins of mud cracking around their edges pocked with hoofprints. He did not see any ducks. The railway followed a direct route. No lazy meandering. He had a plot to hatch. And the movement of his legs was part of its hatching. When he reached the city he left the railway line and made his way anonymously through the streets. He found a quiet spot to rest by the lagoon in the Victory Memorial Gardens. He watched the setting sun turn the surface of the lagoon green, fading quickly to black. Peahens chased each other between the floating water lilies. Gold flashes of carp beneath the surface. People passing through the gardens ignored him, or else gave him a wide berth. They had a reputation, these gardens. He watched the yellow streetlights flicker on; the headlights of passing traffic brighten as night was accomplished. He warmed himself by the eternal flame in the war memorial. The sounds of powerful engines grumbled up and down the main street. Tyres squealed. Mosquitoes found him. He passed the time by swatting them. Collected them in a little pile. When he felt it was late enough he rose and began his determined march out of town. Passing by the Friday night clamour of the pubs. The growls of argument. No one gave him a second glance. He felt invisible. The smells of the hamburger vans made him slow down and salivate.

The business district disappeared behind him. He moved down Travers Street, past the fragrant Turf Club. He approached the council pound over the vacant lots that surrounded it. A few goats were penned in the outer yard. A cow. The fence lines were marshalled by skinny eucalypts. There were no houses within cooee. He had no idea of the time, but it seemed to be the right time. There was again a dismal yapping, which increased in tempo at the first *snick* Edgar's wire-cutters made against the first strand of Cyclone mesh surrounding the compound. Hanging from a tree branch was a large cage with a sulphur-crested cockatoo inside it. It leaned over to him as he passed and spoke:

'Hello.'

Edgar did not deign to reply.

There was a change in the rhythm of the barking. The moon was there on the wire. Edgar cut the inner fence from top to bottom, before peeling it apart like a silver scar, ribs opened up. Inside, across the shadows of the yard and within a long row of cages he recognised his dogs, and they recognised him. There were dozens of other dogs, fifty or more, whose new frenzy at his presence was gloriously deafening.

'Quiet now, dorgs.'

No neighbours' lights went on. No cars cruised past. No fortuitously passing midnight pedestrians.

Edgar moved past their enclosure to the cats. All quiet in there. Taking a pair of bolt-cutters from his knapsack he snipped the padlocks from the cages. They did not want to come out, so fierce was the noise from the nearby dogs.

'Come orn, yer stupid cats.'

He drove them all towards the gate, kicking kitty litter and drinking dishes everywhere. They hesitated at the exit, but Edgar's flailing arms and feet drove them out into the night. He gave the lazy ones a boot in the bum. He had to show them the hole in the perimeter fence, where they hesitated before sprinting past him. Others found their own way over. He did not see them all go. They fled into the darkness, beneath buildings, seeking safety up trees. Edgar gave them a good head start while the dogs threw themselves at the wire. Rex and Bex licked his fingers frantically through the mesh. He had never seen so many dogs. Finally he cut the padlock and released the bolt. The place reeked of shit. He opened the bolt of each kennel in the compound. Some of the gates were flung open in his face. The noise did not let up for a moment. They ran everywhere. Into the cats' enclosure and out again. Several of his own dogs leapt on him, then ran off. He watched them go — the staffy, the bully, the Afghan, the mongrel pups, their mother, all the others that he had not named. Even the silky stopped for a sniff, chased its tail in excitement for a moment, and then ran off. Outside the cages they charged around every inch of the perimeter fence. It was like the crowd on a footy ground after a match. As he worked he found himself singing a little song:

'Ivy's in the cellar
By Glory can't you smell her
With snot *dribbling down her nose*
Dribbling down her nose to her toes.'

Or was it Sophie? He was remembering his girl. One of them chewed her nails. Edgar nibbled his quicks.

The dogs were more chaotic and more organised than the cats. Within seconds they had found the hole in the fence and jumped through it. He did not bother to rope any of them. They deserved a bit of a run after being cooped up.

'Garn.'

Only the sound of their barking remained in the night.

At the back of the last enclosure Edgar discovered, with a sigh of sadness, the three-legged Labrador lying on its side. It was cold and stiff. Dead as a dodo. He kneeled by its side, patted its granite head.

'You was a good dorg,' he said, in what was nearly silence.

As he passed the cage hanging in the tree the cockatoo leaned towards him and spoke:

'Hello.'

'Hello, yer stupid fuck.'

Edgar opened the door of the cage, but did not shake the bird out.

He left the pound. The cow still as a statue in the far corner of the front yard, eyes alert to all the fuss it had seen. He headed along the back streets out of town. Occasionally faint barking drifted over the tops of dark houses. He crossed the rickety old Hampden Bridge over the river. The sliver of moon was now higher in the sky, but even without it he was confident he could find his way to the shearing shed. He felt happy. He felt he'd done good. The long grass on the northern side of the river brushed against his legs as he moved through it. He was filled with the private triumph of the breakout, and he did not notice how low the Southern Cross had come in the sky until the familiar shape of the shed rose from the grass. He raised his hands up against the light of the stars. It was impossible to distinguish where the sound of mopokes came from and as he approached the shed two of the dogs ran out to greet him.

In the pitch darkness he recognised by touch that his companions were two of the grown pups. They slept in the old fleeces, snuggled up for warmth. The wings of an owl ruffled in the rafters, before settling. It was used to them now. He thought it was a boobook.

They dreamed in spasms of running and of long grass. By dawn the owl was gone. Before the new day was broken, two more of the dogs had returned. The smell of lanolin was comforting for them all, and they sniffed every corner of the shed. In one of the stalls he found Meacham's empty rum bottle. And his hat. It was a good hat. Over the course of the day three more dogs returned, including Rex and Bex and the battle-scarred bull mastiff with tattered ears. There was riotous reunion between them all, rolling over the ground, grovelling and wrestling, the mock battles for status, running like mad things around the shed. Edgar cuffed them over the ears and flung them away when they jumped on him. If they combined their efforts sometimes they were able to knock him down, but they never bit him too hard, and if they did he kind of liked it. Edgar knew how to do battle with dogs. When he threw them off they sprang back and in the manner of this play, reasserting their pecking order, the days passed.

A few mornings later the old silky wandered back on short, weary legs, then a couple of the mongrels, so that Edgar had nearly half his pack. He thought this a pretty fair ratio and expected to pick up more the next time they went to town. However when this would be he did not know. Town. Some of the shopkeepers, it seemed, were cranky with him.

'The thing is, dorgs,' he said to them, 'looks like we'll have to keep our heads down fer a bit.'

They tried to live as best they could on what they hunted, which was not much. The possums had all been cleared out of the ceiling. So too the rats. Underneath a sheet of roofing iron they found a hibernating snake, whose sluggish movements at being disturbed did it no good at all. However a snake or two did not go far amongst those hungry dogs. The bull mastiff ran down a young wild pig which, after the thrill of the chase, Edgar finished off with the knife. His heart pumped fit to bust. He found the curl of the tusks very interesting, but Edgar, like the silky, was a fussy eater. He did not like pig.

They managed to kill an old wether out in a distant paddock, far from the shed. After letting them devour what they could out there in the open, Edgar-the-butcher sliced and chopped up the remains of the carcass and, stuffing the bloody chunks into his knapsack, carried it back to the shed. One of the dogs rolled in the offal. The sheep lasted them a few days, but the fact was, they were growing leaner. Their meals came further and further apart, but Edgar would not leave the protection of the shed. The ribs of the dogs began to feel more prominent to his touch, but it was touch at least that kept them together. Sometimes the dogs turned on one another, and Edgar had to separate them with a stick or his boots. The silky, being the oldest, had the sense to stay out of these squabbles. Once one of the younger dogs snapped viciously at Edgar, drawing blood. Edgar gave it a good kick in the slats, and when it snarled it almost spoke with a human voice.

Days passed. Rainy days and not-so-rainy. Sunny days and not-so. Edgar knew it was inevitable they would have to return to town. He also knew that they would have to target one of the other supermarkets. Mr Ashcroft had poisoned the well for sure. That snake had probably been in cahoots with Kate Shoebridge all along. There had been a conspiracy against him: the dog-catcher had probably been in on it as well. And didn't Ivy Cornish know the dog-catcher? They set off happily with a cloud of flies hitching a lift on the knapsack. In a couple of hours they arrived at the river and turned in the direction of the bridge. They might have swum across, but Edgar knew the silky did not really like the water, and there was no reason that he could think of to save time. Time, as always, belonged to him whether he wanted it or not.

The levee on the far side of the river shielded them from the gaze of anyone passing. But there was no one. He tossed clods of dirt into the alarming calm of the river, watching the ripples widen into rings that floated downstream. Their speed belied the smooth surface of the water. Occasionally paddocks came right down to the water's edge, but on this side they ambled through grass and weeds. The dogs bounded off through the roots of willow trees and she-oaks, snuffling into every hole. Edgar dawdled behind, his feet flattening the grass. His stomach grumbled with hunger. He found himself savouring the prospect of a chicken. A cormorant shook itself loose from the exposed knuckles of a river gum's roots. Over the treetops further along the river crows burst into the air. Somewhere a duck quacked. Or was it a dog?

In time, for it was not sudden, Edgar realised that he was alone. The dogs had run far ahead. He heard their faint barking, growling. He quickened his pace through the grass, calling out:

'Dorgs.'

Through the trees he saw them and was reassured. They'd found something. They'd stopped running and were feeding, snapping at each other. He saw they were eating quickly. Edgar ran up to them.

'What have yez gort?' he barked at them.

The bull mastiff turned its head and snarled at him. Growled at him, the ungrateful bastard.

'Growl at me, will yer.'

He tried to beat them apart with his knapsack, which had the hatchet in it. They would not part. He took the hatchet out and flailed at them with the blunt edge of the head.

'Git orf of it.'

The axe head cracked on something.

One of the pups yelped and ran off through the grass. Edgar jumped into the midst of the pack, whacking at anything that moved, until finally the dogs yielded and moved back, teeth bared and snarling, as Edgar looked down at the carnage of what they had found and recognised the hands.

THREE

'All stand.'

The clerk of courts rose and there followed a general shuffling of chair legs and shoe leather. The judge, resplendent in his wig and red robe, entered from the side door and sat on his velvet cushion. So too the retinue of court personnel, the prosecuting attorneys of the DPP, their lackeys; the defence barrister, Ms Henry, and her solicitor; the sundry public and a bevy of journalists. (I read all the details later in the trial transcripts.) So too rose the custodial bailiff and court security warden who had stools behind the accused, who was seated in the dock. The Sydney diocese of the NSW Supreme Court was in session. Edgar did not stand. He was asleep. In fact, according to one of the tabloid journalists, he was obscenely asleep. His head lolled back. His jaw agape, giving the entire room full view of the inside of his mouth. Its toothless, naked gate. His tonsils. His scar. No need to look further for the mark, if such a mark helped explain the inexplicable. Such comments found their way into the simplifications of proceedings. Indeed some of them were so keen to impress editors as to invoke, in one weekend magazine supplement, a quasi-phrenological analysis of the prisoner's whole demeanour, trying hard to rationalise the machinations of fate.

Edgar snored. His adenoids spluttered loudly and occasionally he woke himself with a start. The jury stared at him in disbelief from across the room. This had been Edgar's pattern of behaviour throughout the trial. To fall asleep; to snore; to wake suddenly; to rant and rave. The nomenclature, the courtroom idiom was a complete mystery to him. How could it not be? It was like some mad barking. The minutiae of forensic analysis, or the testimony of expert witnesses, it was grisly and clinical. It didn't seem to bother the journalists, beyond its capacity to claim a headline. It was all gobbledegook to Edgar, who for the most part sat fast asleep, his ugly gob wide open. Snorting. Like a grampus. If you please. Your Honour.

Judge Crowther ordered the prisoner awake — to cease that snoring and pay attention. Poke him, if you must. There was important business at hand. The bailiff prodded Edgar, who, starting awake, blinking at the light, immediately leapt the polished rail of the dock in front of him, knocking the microphone askew, and attacked the prothonotary who appeared before him. He knocked the clerk down and bolted for the exit. People screamed. Bailiffs and custodial officers ran from two doors. Code One. They surrounded Edgar and clasped him, jumping as one, like pals celebrating victory at a sporting contest.

There was a short recess.

Down in the holding cells they gave Edgar a few in the breadbasket to be going on with. It took a lot of them to hold him down.

When court resumed the prisoner was suitably restrained in cuffs and shackles. Edgar saw, or dreamed he saw, sitting at the back of the public gallery, the woman he'd seen at the mother's funeral, who said she was his sister. It was.

My mother had taken a great deal of interest in proceedings concerning her brother since being informed of them by a journalist at her doorstep. My father said he did not care if I knew or not, he had washed his hands of his crazy brother-in-law. I was old enough to make up my own mind, and if I had any sense I'd forget about him too, past being past. I was still at school then, and did not care about anything much beyond the range of my own pimples, but I remember my curiosity being tweaked by talk of this shameful uncle — hadn't I met him? — from the backwoods. I remember the tension this caused in our household, as an obsession took hold in my mother's heart.

I did not go with her. Why? I had places to be and girls to chase.

Lynne tried to remain hidden from him, seated behind other members of the public. The judge asked if Edgar was now persuaded to attend to what was going on around him, to proceedings that impinged on him particularly.

'Do you understand me, Mr Hamilton?'

'Eh?'

'The seriousness of the matter that faces you.'

Edgar belched loudly. People in the gallery had given up sniggering. Edgar struggled against his chains for a while, then, as testimony proceeded, fell asleep again.

Sometimes it seemed to those observing that he pretended to sleep.

Sometimes he sang. Or whistled. Or made bird noises. Or clucked like a chicken. Or quacked. At other times he did push-ups, or squats in the dock, or yawned loudly, baring the full extent of his cleft discrepancy to the jury. Or else he farted. Or threw pencils and jelly beans about the court, including at his own defence counsel. Ms Henry couldn't control him. He showed his muscles and posed like a statue for the court artist who was sketching him. The early humour of all this had vanished. He seemed to have no idea of the image he was presenting to anyone else in the room.

He either slept or he raged. Even with his wrists handcuffed he managed to clout one of the wardens who was escorting him to his place in the dock. Ms Henry, the Legal Aid-appointed defence counsel, argued, basically, that the accused had no idea what was going on around him. He was clearly unfit to plead, and unfit to be tried. Full stop. The prosecutor argued the converse, that Edgar knew perfectly well what he was doing, disrupting proceedings in order to exculpate himself in the only way he knew how. His behaviour was ingenuously counterfeit.

Edgar suspected the day outside was windy, although he had not felt the wind for some time. Light pulsed in from the high windows, throwing swift rags of shadow across the panelling of the walls. Clouds on the move.

'Mr Hamilton,' the judge said to Edgar suddenly, at yet another submission from the defence, 'do you understand what issue is at stake here?'

'Eh?'

'Do you know what we're talking about today?'

'How would I know what yer talkin' about, yer great goose?'

'Shh,' said the defence.

'We are trying to determine whether or not you are fit to plead to the charge.'

'I'm fit, lookit me, look how muscly and healthy I am.'

When Edgar's outbursts continued Judge Crowther, whom Edgar had variously addressed as 'a maggot', 'a nong', 'a shitbag', 'a drongo', 'a infestation', as well as 'a great goose', was not impressed. According to trial transcripts 'he also spent considerable time talking loudly about earwigs'. Crowther adjudicated on the side of the prosecution. Nothing new had been introduced to show that he was any less fit to plead than on the first day of the trial, nor indeed since the time of his arrest. The fitness hearing, conducted previously, and presided over by Judge Crowther, had determined as much. In fact he had found that the prisoner's behaviour was 'merely an attempt to assoil himself through calculated mendacity'. Edgar was fit to plead. The trial would continue.

The incontrovertible facts were discussed in detail. The media loved those. My father too, from a distance, had a morbid I-told-you-so curiosity about the whole lurid affair; my mother a more complex emotion. The incontrovertible facts were of no consolation to Aileen Meacham, wife of the victim. She had lost a husband. Under terrible circumstances, it must be said, the judge elaborated. The newspapers seized upon his comments, even though she was quoted as saying, 'He ripped me off blind'. The local community hadn't been so galvanised since the disappearance over a dozen years ago of young ... what was her name? And hadn't the accused and his old man been questioned over that incident? The perpetrator of such a gruesome and callous, vicious and frenzied ... Never to be released ... Justice seen to be done ... Capital punishment ...

Strong words, boyo.

Probationary Officer Bewley described how Edgar had been arrested at a derelict shearing shed, where he had surrounded himself, and was defended by, numerous savage dogs. Police had had to shoot some of them. There were thirteen dogs all told, and three of these were pregnant. The accused was charged at that time with resisting arrest and escaping lawful custody.

Would you mind telling the court exactly how he escaped lawful custody, Officer Bewley? asked Ms Henry.

By wrenching his arm out of my grasp.

Were you squeezing the arm tightly?

Yes, I was, so as to prevent the possibility of an escape.

Then it's hardly surprising that he wrenched his arm out of your grasp.

Relevance, your Honour, where is this line of questioning going?

It was said that Edgar tried to crawl off through the grass. A gun was held to his head. He was later charged with the murder of Dennis Meacham, who also went by the alias of Wayne Walsh. His blood was found on Edgar's clothes. Indeed, Meacham's dried blood was found clotted in the hair of the muzzles of some of the dogs at the shed. His watch was found in Edgar's knapsack. His hat was found on Edgar's head! This physical evidence was beyond dispute. The victim was purportedly unknown to the prisoner. Edgar struggled against his chains. The fact that the victim had a criminal history, which his wife later described in a glossy magazine article as 'small time in every way', did not ameliorate the seriousness of the charge which, while not falling into the worst category of homicide, was still a *vicious* and *frenzied*, *gruesome* and *callous attack*. (Fine emotive words for the jury to consider.) Death had occurred before the macabre mauling of the dogs, the motive of which could only be guessed at: an accident perhaps? The prosecutor speculated further: a clumsy attempt to disguise the cause of death coupled with, after the event, an attempt to remove, or even *rid* the body to a better place of concealment.

This was laughed down as frivolous supposition by the lawyer who seemed most to be on Edgar's side, a woman wearin' duds. Edgar knew they were all working together. It was another conspiracy. The goose in the wig, the squawking eagles, and the rest of them, all in league together.

The cause of Meacham's death was a cut throat.

Much later on, when I was asked to look over these files, there were questions Lynne, my mother, wanted answered. My initial brief from Mr Pennington was: 'Find out what you can and we'll take it from there.' I took some transcripts home with me for the weekend.

Was it possible to distinguish between the type of injury that might be sustained by a knife, such as the type of knife found in the accused's knapsack, and injuries that may or may not have been the result of a vicious and frenzied attack, injuries caused perhaps by canine incisors?

Yes, it was.

The severity of the wound to the right side of the victim's neck had transected the right common carotid artery, the right vertebral artery and the right jugular vein. Also the oesophagus, trachea, and cut the cervical spinal cord. A dog's tooth could not do that.

Could a hatchet?

No, not a hatchet. Other injuries, made by the hatchet, were glancing blows caused after death.

An accident perhaps?

From the photos, horrific as they were, how was it possible to deduce this?

It was possible. The wound was deeper than a bite.

It was not possible, however, to determine whether there were any additional puncture wounds to the abdomen, other than those caused by the dogs. Stabs, or thrusts, for instance, rather than cuts?

No.

Could such injuries as described in the coroner's report have been caused by the type of knife found in the accused's possession?

It's possible.

Possible?

Possible.

An effort had been made to clean the knife.

That's right, although the blood remaining on it was not that of the victim.

Ms Henry, the defence counsel, put it to the jury that the accused, who it must be remembered was still innocent until proven otherwise, had merely stumbled upon the body of Dennis Meacham, who had been murdered by person or persons unknown. For reasons known only to himself the accused had decided to relocate the body to its site of discovery, which would explain the presence of Meacham's blood on his person.

It was the prosecutor's turn to scoff. Edgar didn't like the look of him. What about the watch? he reminded the jury, or the hat, which had been identified by Aileen Meacham. The watch had a distinctive engraving on the back.

Yes, she could recall what it said. She'd thought he'd lost it gambling.

No attempt was made to suggest that Edgar take the stand to answer these and other questions, including his whereabouts at the time of the crime. Edgar was picking his nose. Ms Henry brought to the jury's attention the fact that an accused person's refusal to testify in no way implies an admission of any sort — there is no obligation. Judge Crowther endorsed this point.

Several motorists then took the oath and swore how they had seen the accused with all his savage dogs, dressed as a cowboy, frightening sheep in a paddock, on or about the day the murder took place.

Next, a photographer from the *Daily Advertiser* testified how one of these savage dogs tried to take a chunk out of him down by the river as he was attempting to get out of his vehicle whilst on assignment to cover a story for his editor. No, the pictures weren't very clear. Sorry.

Mr Leonard Ashcroft of Coles supermarket took the stand and told how Edgar had menaced him out of a very considerable sums' worth of canned groceries, particularly pet food, (itemised exhibit submitted). This, in his opinion, was tantamount to extortion.

Then Doug Medson, a local businessman, swore how, at school, the accused had slashed the back of his knee with a razor blade. This had been found to be the documented cause for his expulsion.

A forensic pathologist established beyond doubt that Mr Meacham's blood type, O positive, and the stains found on Edgar's trousers, specifically the knees, were not only compatible, but genetically identical. A murmur rippled across the gallery. Edgar jumped up, forced to hunch over by the shackles, and shouted out:

'Yez all fuckin' dorgs. I'll tell yez nothin',' and barked, before he was roughly flung back in his pillory.

There was an adjournment for lunch.

Down in the cells Edgar sacked the solicitor who had been appointed for him. He appeared to view the whole situation in a most humorous light. He hung laughing from the bars of his cell like a monkey. It was only with reluctance that he was persuaded to reinstate her.

I spoke with Maureen Henry some years later when she was senior partner with O'Donahue, Bayeh, Gold and Henry. She remembered Edgar clearly. I did not tell her then that he was my uncle. I was merely a young go-getter in a suit interested in jurisprudential history. I had a note from Pennington. She told me how she had borrowed a stool and sat down outside the bars. They wouldn't let her sit inside the cell.

Listen, she'd put it to him, perhaps Meacham had been killed accidentally, would he agree that perhaps that was what happened?

Edgar would not agree.

'An' what do they mean I din't know him?'

Perched on her stool, out in the corridor, Maureen Henry paused. Officers of the court walked past.

She continued: perhaps there had been some provocation on the deceased's part, an unreciprocated advance — an assault — Meacham did have a criminal record after all ... extenuating circumstances?

'No,' said Edgar, 'nothin' like that.'

'Then why, for God's sake, did you touch the body? I don't want to put words in your mouth but, Mr Hamilton, how can I help you? What do you want me to do? Did he attack you?'

'I din't touch the body,' said Edgar. 'Why would I do that?'

'So you did see the body?'

'When I beat the dorgs orf.'

'Did you touch it?'

'Nuh. I din't. I din't want to.'

'There's blood on your pants.'

'The body touched me.'

'He was alive?'

'I dunno the name of it.'

'Did he say anything?'

Edgar laughed.

'What did you do then?'

'I runned orf.'

'Where to?'

'Through the grass.'

'What about the hat?'

'I needed a hat.'

'The watch?'

'It's a good watch. It were all that were left lyin' there.'

'Did you know him?'

'In the shed. Somethin' about the stars. The tripod liked him. Mum's the word.'

All of this was off the record.

For all that, it was the most cogent she had found him. The fact that the two may have known each other, she felt, would have played straight into the prosecution's hands, providing opportunity to establish motive. So she decided for better or worse to keep that information to herself. After lunch it was hypothesised that Meacham may have been killed in the shearing shed where Edgar had been arrested. It resembled an ossuary, or an abattoir, with carcasses, bones of heifers, sheep, wallabies, pigs, in the shade beneath the shed. Bloody fleeces strewn on the floor. Also hundreds of empty, rusting dog food tins in a small pyramid. Plus Meacham's hat. Small bloodstains found there also proved to be a positive match with the victim's genetic profile.

Then what?

So then he had carried the body to his car and driven it to a desolate spot along the riverbank.

But Edgar was a derelict, argued Ms Henry. He had no vehicle, nor a licence to drive any vehicle.

Ah, but that had not stopped him driving an unregistered vehicle through the emergency doors of the Base Hospital in August of 1986.

But had that not been an emergency, at least in the accused's state of mind, which is precisely the point at issue, the accused's state of mind, and his fitness to plead?

Objection.

Sustained. Accused's state of mind is not at issue here.

None of this was looking good for Edgar.

The defence counsel paused a moment to examine the moist, snorting cavern that was the mouth of the accused, the tongue resting in the vacancy where the teeth should have been. Another adjournment was requested to clarify a few points of law. The jury was sent from the room. Edgar was lifted rudely under the arms ('Wha? Wha?') before being shunted down to the holding cells. Counsel approached the bench. Ms Henry intimated: please take a look at him, your Honour, he clearly doesn't know what's going on. He should be regarded as a forensic patient.

Rubbish, all that was being requested, it seemed to his Honour, was to reventilate an issue which had previously been determined. Judge Crowther reminded counsel of *R v Chad*, which was particularly pertinent, and of the early verdict of *R v Dyson* where the defendant, a deaf mute you might recall, was indicted in 1831 for infanticide. After learning that the woman had always been deaf and dumb, the jury adjudged her to be mute by the visitation of God. However, by making signs to a friend, she was able to deny the accusations. The friend had instructed her in the dumb alphabet, but she was not accomplished enough to form words, let alone coherent sentences. It was impossible for her to comprehend the more complex aspects of jurisprudence. Yet, like Ms Henry's client, she had not been regarded as insane, and was therefore, at the end of the day, fit to stand trial, and was punished accordingly. Food for thought, Ms Henry. Food for cogitation.

Indeed, your Honour.

The McNaughton Rules for criminal insanity did not apply. *R v Chad* was a different kettle of fish altogether.

On the street outside the courtroom, before the cameras, Aileen Meacham told how her husband, himself a troubled man, had also been a gentle man, a nice man, a decent father, 'even if he did rip me off blind'. Her eyes were red and puffy. He did not deserve to wind up ... She only hoped that the full weight of the law saw fit to administer the same justice and mercy that Hamilton had shown her husband ... She was led away by women's magazine reporters.

Victim statements were submitted to the court. Strong words.

In his summing up the next morning Judge Crowther said that the incontrovertible facts were well supported by a wealth of circumstantial evidence, not least of which was an obvious lack of contrition on the part of the accused. He would therefore be directing the jury toward the only logical conclusion permitted by the laws of evidence.

Down in the holding cell there were four walls. There was also a bunk; a bucket to relieve himself in; a bright fluorescent tube blazing in the ceiling; no windows. Edgar stared at the walls. He stared at the words gouged on them that he could not decipher.

Night senior reported that he was whimpering like a pup.

* * *

Next morning, as soon as the door was opened, Edgar sprang out and attacked the warder with his shoe. He knocked the man off his feet and bit his arm. It was a struggle to get him back in the cell, but eventually they did, before dousing their scratches with bleach. So Edgar was not present for the allocutus — not that it would have mattered, by all accounts — when Judge Crowther returned from his chambers and the clerk rose to announce:

'All stand.'

Nor was he present when the jury was asked: 'In respect of count one, how say you?'

Nor when juror number one handed the note to the clerk who read the verdict and the word 'Guilty' was heard in that room.

After the outbursts had died down, the judge ordered the prisoner to be brought forth to hear the verdict and receive sentence. Officers were dispatched. Did counsel for the defence have any pre-sentencing submissions that might constitute grounds for an adjournment?

Plenty, your Honour, objected Ms Henry.

One by one, these were duly noted and rejected, noted and rejected.

Your client, Ms Henry, could not be said to have helped his own cause, he was in this instance his own worst enemy. Where is your client, by the way?

Much time had passed. The prisoner did not appear. Instead, one of the grim-looking bailiffs with a Band-Aid across his nose handed a note to the clerk, who read it, turning, affronted almost, first to Ms Henry, then to the judge, and whispered across the bench.

The judge turned his hoary ear. 'I beg your pardon. What do you mean, he cannot be manhandled? I want him out here. This is not a bus stop. Manhandle away.'

Further whispering.

'Going *what*?'

And: 'What did you say?'

At that moment, with great dramatic effect, the door to the holding cells in the basement banged open. The officers all stepped back. The prisoner, shackles still on his feet (he'd slept in them), but with arms free, rattled slowly up the steps to the dock and stood looking out at the court.

'I've sacked the bitch,' he said. 'I'm gunna repersent meself.'

With that Edgar saluted theatrically. He sat at his own command. No one touched him. The judge pursed his lips. While the members of the public in the gallery did not immediately understand, a collective sense of comprehension gradually spread throughout the courtroom, that Edgar was sitting there smeared in his own excrement. No one would beat or manhandle him now. No one dared lay a finger on him. He sat there rather proudly. There was stunned silence for several moments. Ms Henry remembers shaking her head.

The verdict was repeated, which had much less impact in the room than had been anticipated. The judge adjusted his wig. There seemed to be no point in delaying proceedings. Everyone had busy schedules. No point coming back here tomorrow. A tragic set of circumstances. A sentence was announced — in the context of quoting *Regina v Chad*, noting few educational prospects, poor prospect for rehabilitation — constructed in the following way: twenty-six years penal servitude in a maximum security facility with a minimum fixed term of nineteen years. Full stop.

FOUR

After he was hosed down in the yards, by all accounts the custodial officers in their starched powder blue bundled him, handcuffed, into the back of the transit truck. They did this with practised, stony indifference. The interior was small and cramped, segmented into tinier compartments. It smelled of urine. Edgar was paired with a man who would not speak. He looked sideways at the hook of the man's nose, trying (why not?) to elicit a response, but the man would not acknowledge anything. For the most part he kept his eyes closed. The windows were blacked out. Thin slits of light cut across the top of the glass so that he had to stand if he wanted to look out. At what? Buildings and traffic. He'd never seen buildings so tall as the Sydney skyscrapers before. A few press photographers had taken snaps of him as he stepped into the truck. The hook-nosed man had looked at him then. Although it was a hot day the heaters had been switched on, warm air blasting down on him as at the entrance to supermarkets.

He was shaken to the bones by the time the truck arrived at the prison several hours later. Although Edgar had little notion of time — it felt as though the whole day had been spent juddering and jarring along the road — it was preferable to the unbearable tedium of the courtroom and the trial. He had almost gone mad with boredom, but he never told the bastards anything. That was the way. He was glad he would not have to go back there again.

Standing to gaze out the window slit, Edgar saw the great mandible of the gate fold and rise up. The truck limped over the last speed hump and rolled into the echoing cavern of the gatehouse, darkening as the gate unfolded behind them, sound of the engine growing louder all around. Inside the second gate, between two towering walls, Edgar could see through the wire mesh into the prison proper. He caught a fleeting glimpse of people playing tennis.

In the reception yard the motor cut out and Edgar listened to the metallic ticking of the engine as the truck settled. The door was opened. Edgar and hook-nose, along with four others from the other compartments, were hustled into a large holding cell. It was bigger than the cells at the courthouse. There was a stainless steel toilet without a seat. Nothing else.

Edgar was perfunctorily strip-searched. How he may have felt about this was of no interest to anyone else present. He simply had to obey. He was told to dress in the standard green prison garb and was given a bundle of spare clothes. Also sheets, pillowslips, a pair of running shoes plus laces, a plastic cup, a plastic plate, a plastic knife and fork, a toothbrush, a green jacket which he wouldn't need until winter, though he was told to look after it as he wouldn't get another unless he paid for it himself. The officers behind the counter grinned. They gave him two plastic tubs. From now on, everything he owned must fit within these tubs. Edgar looked at their blank emptiness. They were bigger than his knapsack. All that room. All those possibilities. How would he ever fill them?

His photograph was taken. He was given a MIN number; assigned a unit and a cell. Two rovers were summoned by radio to escort him. Up the corridor from reception they passed an open door. It led into a small chapel with two rows of polished wooden pews. Edgar thought of the gleaming woodwork of

the courthouse and hurried past. He followed the
warders. There were several steel doors and heavy
gates to unlock. They had great dangling bunches of
keys at their belts to choose from, locking them
again as they passed through. In the compound
several inmates watched Edgar walk past in his new
running shoes, with his tubs. Yes, there were tennis
courts. People playing tennis. Others sat around on
concrete benches. Using them to exercise. Step-ups,
or elaborate push-ups. Still others were jogging
around the perimeter fencing of the tennis courts;
around the circumference of the inner walls; around
other smaller portions of the compound on selected
pathways of their own devising. Endless exercise. To
Edgar they appeared to be making do.

There was a circle of lawn with a garden bed in
the middle of the bottom compound. A man with a
hoe was scarifying weeds. Inside the unit Edgar was
shown, rather than introduced to, the wing officer in
charge. He was Mister O'Neil and was to be
addressed at all times as Mister O'Neil. Mister
O'Neil took Edgar's ID card, wrote down a few
particulars. He placed it in a rack displaying all the
other residents of the wing — all the smiling,
scowling, indolent, butchered faces. Edgar followed
another officer, who unlocked a cell door for him.

'Home.'

Edgar entered and the door was slammed behind him with an iron echo and a great resounding click.

Like the cellar of the courthouse Edgar's cell had four walls. They had been scrubbed once, long ago, but here and there the ghosts of old graffiti showed through. The contents of Edgar's two tubs did not go a long way to adding the homey touches he had noticed through the open doors of neighbouring cells. There was a narrow bunk taking up a third of the floor space. A toilet, lidless. A shower. He tried the taps. They worked. Hot water, no, warm. A hand basin. A plate of stainless steel had been riveted to the wall and buffed until it assumed the purpose of a mirror, with random distortions where previous residents had thumped the metal and dented it. He examined his own blurred reflection:

'Well, yer fucked now,' he said to himself.

There was a small table also attached to the wall, and a plastic chair. There was a *window*. Edgar examined all these things, his possessions, over and over. Would possessions alone sustain a life?

He had a lot of time, not only on that first day, to stare at the walls. He heard the garbled announcement ordering the return of tennis racquets, and the imminence of muster. He heard the inmates return to the unit. Someone opened his door and gave him a sandwich. Then the sequential thudding of each door as it was slammed home for the night, even though it was still mid-afternoon. A long night began. He could yell, he supposed, he could rant and rave, but would anyone take any notice?

Throughout the evening he heard the occasional shouting of voices.

He dreamed of Meacham, the jagged rum bottle raised to the faceless face. They shared the bottle and Edgar held the broken glass to his lips.

In the morning Edgar was wakened by the sound of keys in the lock and the heavy door being opened. When he emerged he had his first look at the man who had slept on the other side of the wall, within a spit of him, and all the others, and they of him. An officer holding a book called their names. They queued for their breakfast. One inmate with tattoos down to the quicks of his fingers handed out fruit and milk. The pear he handed to Edgar was as hard as a bone.

The wing officer, Mr O'Neil, with his smart epaulettes, told him he had to go outside with the others. Men were already jogging in endless circles. It was not raining, although it felt as though it should be. Someone asked him his name.

* * *

Whether it was raining or not, cold or not, hot or not, gradually became the medium by which Edgar began to sense time passing. His name was called three times a day at muster. The doors were locked and unlocked at exactly the same times. Little distinguished the meals. The other inmates complained unceasingly about the awfulness of the food, but Edgar reckoned he had eaten worse and when asked he told them so. The routine had not yet lost its novelty. His two tubs still contained the possibility of multitudes. He had twenty solid pears lined up on his table in varying degrees of readiness, none of them quite ripe enough to eat. They did not rot. Some of the inmates said they had read about Edgar in the paper, the state of his victim. He was notorious. Ed-the-ripper. Towards the end of his first season (it was still warm), the line of pears growing longer on his table (the softer ones confiscated before they might ferment), Mr O'Neil told him he must work.

Birds occasionally flew into the compound — sparrows, currawongs, even a family of plovers. Lone crows pecking through bags of garbage left outside the unit gates at lock-in. Edgar watched them through the finger holes in the grille that covered the bars on his window. Where did they lay their eggs? he wondered. In those months

Edgar hung his jacket over the window to thwart the dawn. In the dimness he created he was able to sleep long and hard. He would have slept all day if he could. Sometimes he did, when the screws locked the gaol down. (*Screws*: Edgar was slowly getting a hang of the new lingo.) Sometimes, if there had been a fight, or a screw got walloped, or a pair of scissors went missing, the entire place would be shut down to punish everyone. It was a strange stasis. There were beatings. There were puerile torments. And now Edgar had been asked to work.

Edgar who had never had a job in his life.

It's either that or the withdrawal of privileges. Edgar went the next day with the other workers to the textiles factory, which was housed behind a solid brick wall running along one side of the gaol. This was a new experience for him. A new room in his mind had been opened, as in a dream — he'd had no idea there was anything on the other side of this wall. The shop floor hummed with the sound of well-oiled machinery, like the language of bees. Sewing machines. There seemed to be hundreds of them stretching across the concrete floor to the wall, although Edgar's sense of quantity was no more reliable than his estimate of time.

An officer put him to work at a vacant machine. What was he supposed to do now? The man working next to him came across.

'Not like this, not like this,' shaking his little finger with its long, ludicrous nail.

He spoke with a thick accent Edgar could not easily understand, though he recognised the hooked nose, the swarthy complexion of the man he had sat next to in the truck the day they had arrived. Edgar mimed driving. The man nodded. Here was a bond. A moment of recognition that was like finding the dogs again after returning to the shearing shed.

But he couldn't bring himself to think of the dogs. That thought was an agony. That thought bit. In his mind all the dogs began to turn to stone.

'Yema,' the man said, pointing to himself, and they shook hands. The man, Yema, turned to the machine. He showed Edgar how to raise the foot so as to feed the material through; how to lower the foot and load the bobbin, how to adjust the tension wheel. He warned Edgar to keep his fingers away from the needle, and that if he broke one he had to get a new needle from the screws. Slowly Edgar began to get the idea. He laughed out loud when the stitches began to appear in a short sharp burst, like a cicatrice in the cloth or, indeed, like the flawed junction in his own lip. Yema, of course, was much faster. He called out encouragement to Edgar, not to let the material bunch up. He inspected Edgar's stitches, holding them close to his eyes, and gave him further tips. By lunchtime Edgar was beginning to get the hang of it. He had enjoyed himself, and thanked Yema for helping him.

'Where yer from?' Edgar asked.

'Pardon?'

'Where do yer come from?'

'Frum Afghanistan.'

'Is that near Wagga?'

Yema laughed. Good joke. Was it? Edgar wondered why. By the end of the day he was humming along with his machine. It was like riding a motorbike. Well, almost. If this was retribution then it was not working. Edgar felt happy. Well, almost. The overseer came and inspected their work, the quality and evenness, tallying what they had accomplished against the quota he had fixed under a clipboard. He nodded to himself. Snipped a few loose hanging dags of cotton. The machines were switched off and fell silent one by one. Only as they were packing up to leave did Edgar speak to the screw, who was wearing rubber gloves with which to pat them down. Edgar began to recognise these commonplace routines.

'What's this for, chief?'

'What?'

'What're we makin' here, chief?'

'Flags.' The overseer looked at him.

'Flags?'

'Flags. Australian flags. If you don't like it you can go down the other end, I've got a vacancy in shrouds.'

'Eh?'

'Shrouds. Coffin linings. Funeral shrouds.'

'I'll stick ter flags.'

Outside Edgar remembered at once the mother's coffin lowering into the earth. Had her body been wrapped in a flag? Yema could not understand all the fuss and delay associated with the rituals of Western burial. Where he came from the sooner they buried the dead in the comfort of the grave, plainly wrapped, on their right-hand side, facing Mecca, the better for everyone. How the Angel of Death must laugh at you Westerners, when he came to collect the souls of the dead in all their pretty finery. Edgar wondered at all this talk of death. Perhaps his own right to live was forfeit, after all he had been born with the cord around his neck, he shouldn't have lived. No no no, Yema sought to explain, the angel in charge of embryos in the womb had been looking after him. God was good. He was meant to live. He had been saved for greater things. Yeah, like sewing flags. Yes, why not? Very patriotic. Yema gleaned a great sense of purpose from futility. It was either that or go mad. Other work came their way, depending on orders. The factory also made clothes; their own clothes; officers' uniforms too — a bonus of three cents for every collar you sewed above the quota. They also sewed surgical gowns and hospital bedsheets. Edgar listened to the rhythm of Yema's voice. If the screw had told Edgar he must work, then work he must. And if he refused? Well, said Yema, lowering his voice, he could always go and join the blacks in the non-workers unit, but he did not recommend that. In fact he shuddered. Life not worth a cigarette paper. So Edgar stayed with flags. He grew to like them, to like his skill in their assembly. He examined the stitching of his own clothes with a new eye.

At its least, work enabled the time to pass from hot to cold, dry to wet.

A sense of balance. He dreamed, or thought he dreamed, of the stone dogs feeding by the river — of him trying to beat them apart with the hatchet — of the mother's voice beneath the pack: *Help me, Eddy, get them off me*. He spluttered awake. If anything would drive him mad, it was those damned grassdogs. Gazing at the paint on the walls, Edgar's thoughts would drift. Occasionally he saw the grass sway and flow with the breeze like the surface of water. And tunnelling beneath it, like a machine or some animal, something burrowing towards him. He watched the rye-grass shudder until whatever it was reached the paint and dispersed and disappeared.

Cold to hot. Wet to dry.

In this context, back when the time was still warm, Yema one day told him that he now had money in his account.

What did he need money for in gaol? Everything was provided. Edgar told his friend that he had money in an account on the outside, but had never seen the need to make much use of it.

'Shh,' hissed Yema, 'never tell people in here that.'

Money could buy all sorts of things, even in gaol. Small luxuries. Yema showed Edgar how to fill in the buy-up form. Tobacco, for example, was worth a week's wages. Edgar did not want tobacco. He wanted to know if he had enough to buy a Paddle Pop? Why yes, more than enough. How much was a Paddle Pop? A Paddle Pop was eighty-one cents, they debited the amount from your account. They also took out TV rental, if you rented a TV, and a percentage went to pay for victims' compensation. Edgar wanted to know how could they compensate the victim when his victim was dead? Well, there was the matter of the family. Yema changed the subject. He didn't want to talk about his victim either.

Yema did not have a TV. Furthermore he admired how Edgar had resisted the mindless soporific of television. The Department sanctioned it. It kept the rabble quiet. It had become a management tool, the way they kept replaying the video movies over and over. Television and methadone. Hang on, Edgar said, I wouldn't mind watching a bit of telly if I had half a chance. No no no my friend, it dulls the mind and stultifies the senses, it makes you submit to the oppressor. The opiate of the Infidel. Edgar snorted at these funny words. Yema could speak five languages and sometimes, for all Edgar could understand, he was speaking them all at once. Edgar waved the buy-up form, did Yema mean to say that according to this bit of paper he could get two Paddle Pops if he wanted?

Yes, that is what it meant.

So Edgar did, and he gave one to Yema. Their tongues leapt at the sweetness of the chocolate. Edgar had almost forgotten the taste. It was marvellous. He wanted another one right now, but was told he would have to wait until next week. Fill in another form. Wait in the queue. In his eyes there was the dawning of a primitive economics.

More so than Edgar, Yema navigated his way methodically through the structured routine of the gaol day, shuffling and obsequious, keeping as low a profile as was humanly possible. He tried to explain this to Edgar. On the straight path over the pit of Hell he was not passing as fast as lightning, or as recklessly as the wind, or as a bird, or a running man, or even a crawling man, but he was inexorably passing. He was presenting the smallest target for Allah's wrath. Where it posed no threat to him he tried to look out for Edgar; helped him when an officer or the loudspeaker barked out an order he could not understand. *He that does a good deed shall be rewarded ten times the like of it*, Yema said.

One day, in the dry months, Yema and Edgar stood in the buy-up line. Edgar had already saved enough to purchase a new kettle, which took pride of place in his tub back in the cell. Clusters of men stood around talking in small groups. Those with purchases moved quickly away from the window. It was dangerous to loiter. An inmate, moving along the line, approached Edgar.

'Smoketherebro?'

'Eh?' Edgar's hearing was never the best, and he was still learning the argot.

'I said — smoke there, bro? Are ya deaf?'

'Don't smoke.'

'What about buyin' us a Paddle Pop then?'

Yema eased himself, ever so gradually, away from Edgar. *And he that does evil shall only be rewarded the like of it.*

'Whafor?'

'You bought one for your Leb friend, why not me?'

'Who?'

'Him, your little Leb mate.'

'Leb?'

'What he is. Where he's from.'

'Is that near Wagga?'

It did not seem unreasonable to Edgar, since he had so much money for Paddle Pops in his account, that he might not lavish his newfound purchasing power upon others. It was the same succour he had received from the supermarkets before they had turned nasty. He gave the young bloke, who was called Indy, a Paddle Pop, and he was most appreciative and the exchange took place in the spirit of brotherhood rather than commerce, although he did not talk to Edgar much during the following days.

Later, when they were alone and were able to find some whispered privacy, Yema said:

'That very bad, to give in to him. There be trouble for you now.'

'I thought he just wanted a icy-pole.'

'Trouble starts with icy-poles. Now he will expect it.'

Edgar was angry he had been tricked. It reminded him of Kate Shoebridge's duplicity. Why was dealing with people always so complicated? So that when the next buy-up day came around, the young man called Indy asked him again for a Paddle Pop, Edgar said no.

'What did you say?'

'Said no. Fuckorf.'

'You stupid as well as ugly? Puttin' me on show in fronta these blokes.'

The blokes were all looking the other way.

'Fuckorf.'

'You're a retard. You're a gronk,' Indy yelled, 'You're a deadset chat.'

'I ain't. I's fit. Judge said I's fit.'

Indy walked away shaking his head. There was general laughter, which was hard to pinpoint. Someone called out 'Good on ya,' but no one wanted to be seen directly siding with Edgar, whose stomach was churning.

The next week, after they had made their purchases, Indy returned with a friend, a man called Otto. Edgar saw that Yema's prediction had come true. If he continued to buy things for others, then it would never stop. He would be a soft target. Edgar made sure he licked his ice cream all over. Yema quietly vanished. Indy had lost all trace of his former brotherhood.

'You owe me one Paddle Pop. And Otto too.'

'Fuckorf,' snarled Edgar through the aberration of his mouth.

'That's not nice, gronk,' said the friend, Otto, standing beside Indy. 'Indy likes Paddle Pops.'

'Not nice comin' from such an ugly gronk,' Indy said.

'Yer fuckin' monkeys,' said Edgar, who had no real feeling for the tension that had prickled through the air. There was silence among the nearby inmates who watched in anticipation of some amusement. The only officers were on the far side of the compound, oblivious.

'Ugly gronks need therapy,' said Indy.

With no sense of propriety, or the proper order of things, Edgar kicked the taller one, Otto, as hard as he could in the knackers, then, as he sagged forward, thrust the dripping ice cream deep into the stunned mouth and, with a shove on the stick, down the man's throat. Indy rained blows on Edgar's head and torso, but Edgar ignored them. They reminded him of a form of human contact, which he had forgotten, that he hadn't felt since the father had been alive.

Indy gripped Edgar's arms, but Edgar was strong and threw him off. Otto spluttered, coughing the icy-pole stick and a gobful of Paddle Pop onto the ground. Then it was on and, as according to the laws of mathematics, Edgar landed fewer blows on them than they landed on him. There was a whirlwind of flailing arms and fists. In their combined efforts Edgar's nose was flattened. Tears sprang to his eyes. They began to get the upper hand. He found himself thinking it was lucky he had already lost his teeth. Still he didn't give up. His knuckles were raw but he kept throwing punches at their bony skulls. In time they got him down and were kicking at his head and body. Again, lucky they were only wearing running shoes. They kicked and stamped at him. Edgar curled into a ball.

'Screws.'

The therapy stopped. Edgar rested on his hands and knees, breathing heavily. By the time he was helped to his feet there were no assailants and no witnesses. Edgar wiped the blood from his nose on the back of his hand.

Who had assaulted him? No idea. How many were there? Dunno. Did he want to press charges? Nup. The screws looked around at the sea of insolent faces.

'Let 'em punch on, chief.'

'Who said that?'

No one owned up. The distraction was over. The buy-up queue moved forward. Yema appeared and helped Edgar back to their unit. He sat on the bed while Edgar cleaned the blood from his face and fists. He looked at the distorted flesh in the distorted mirror, one eye already swelling to close.

'You did that very well, my friend,' Yema said.

'Eh? Why?'

'You put up a valiant effort. You kept honour, yet you let them win.'

'They did win.'

'Now they will leave you alone. You are too much work. If it had been easy they would be back tomorrow. If you had beaten them they would come back with shivs to stab you. But because you did not allow them to win easily, they have kept face.'

'They did win,' Edgar said again, his lips thickening.

'Perhaps, but the important thing you have demonstrated is to make them think you are letting them win. It is a subtle language. Now they will understand there is too much trouble standing over you. It is a good result.'

'A good result, he says,' Edgar mumbled, 'a big tick. Thanks, teach.'

Yema was right. Whenever a stranger approached Edgar in the buy-up queue to ask: 'Smoketherebro?' Edgar now knew the formulaic response with which to throw them off. No, you can't have a smoke, bro, because it's my last one. No, you can't have my watch because it was left to me by my old man in his will. No offence caused. None taken. It would be unreasonable to take a man's last smoke, or a father's watch. To do so would justify retaliation. Therefore the questioner would move on like a wolf down the line to find a softer touch, a new bloke, a youngster. A subtle language.

Edgar's bruises subsided. As they turned from purple to brown to yellow he liked to prod their shrinking tenderness. He lifted his face to the air, or to the grille on his window, and sensed the temperature cooling. It felt with the interminable routine of the gaol that each day was the same day repeated over and over. Sometimes he stared at the wire, at the trees on the hill beyond the outer wall, and wondered how long he would have to stay here, how long this single day went on for. Then he remembered. Yema had worked it out for him: until he was fifty-two years old. He didn't know if it was better or worse to put a figure on it. His lip sometimes curled with longing to climb that hill, to hear twigs snap beneath his feet, imagining the view from the top. He promised he would come straight back down. Then, turning away, he steeled himself, wishing the hill aflame.

Yema, on the other hand, was preoccupied with every fragment into which time could be divided. Time since his last meal. Time until lock-in. Time until Ramadan. Time until the day of his release. Hope.

He had lost his watch. He had lost other things as well, including his prized amulet, the system was run by thieves, but it was his watch that he valued most. The standover men hadn't even had a chance to take it. He was composing a letter to the Ombudsman. The watch had been confiscated from him at the time of his arrest. It had cost a lot of money and he wanted it back, or else be compensated for its true monetary value. There was no use denying that officers of the Department had stolen it. Such a handsome watch as his would clearly be attractive to the underpaid and corrupt servants of the State.

'But yer've already got a watch.'

'This is another watch,' Yema held up his wrist, 'worth nothing. A frippery. You must help in my composition to the Ombudsman to instigate the inquiry that will restorate my watch to me.'

'Eh? But I can't write.'

'You know how Australians think. What Australian turn of speech might appeal to the Ombudsman, or is it more better to say Ombudswoman?'

After scratching his chin Edgar said:

'Shit, I dunno.'

This letter was an ongoing concern for Yema. It went through many drafts.

'You know,' he suggested one day to Edgar, 'you could get the Department to provide you with some improved teeth.'

'New teeth?'

'New improved ones. It is your right. It is only just. It will help you to chew the meat more better.'

'Like a dorg, eh?'

'Like a man.'

Sometimes Yema prayed with the other Muslims, Lebanese, Iraqis, Aboriginal converts, at special festivals and on holy days, but usually he kept to himself. They were younger, and despite their language he had little in common with them. Time outside his pathway from cell to sewing machine and back, was time he disliked, when he felt vulnerable. He only wished to be left alone to do, as they say, his own gaol.

One day, when the weather was cooling, with flecks of sleet in the air, Mr O'Neil, the wing officer, summoned Edgar to the officers' station behind its reinforced perspex. A parcel had arrived for him. A large parcel. A big heavy box containing no less than a television, and a doona.

'Who give me this?' he asked.

'Fucked if I know, Ed.'

He carried it back to his cell. Yema read the card, which they found at the bottom of the box and showed the picture of the moon rising over a grass paddock. *For the winter*, it said. The return address had been torn off the envelope.

'Who send me this?'

Yema read the card for him.

'*From Lynne*,' he said, 'Who is this?'

Edgar had to think: 'My sister.'

Despite diagnosis and a cycle of treatment and remission my mother remained passionately concerned with Edgar's situation. She spoke to me of him as I was finishing school and deciding what to do with my prospects. I did not see why she cared about that weirdo loser. Hadn't he wiped dog slobber on me? There'd been ugly photos of him in the paper.

'There but for the grace of God, Tony,' she had said. 'Remember that.'

She did what she could, but she was not a wealthy woman. She was settling her ghosts. Illness had inflamed her. My father drew a line in the sand as far as contributing financially to the comfort and wellbeing of a convicted criminal, let alone this cockamamie idea of hiring a lawyer. She was only just getting better herself, and now this. He buckled under the strength of her conviction. Her sense of injustice at disease had found a focus in her brother. Since the deaths of her parents, those wizened old prunes, she had felt a weight like no other being lifted from her. She owed Edgar something. It was my mother's crusade from the start.

I did not want to listen to them argue any more, so I went out. I had a gram of hash in my pocket, and an uncle called Edgar. No one could tell me what I didn't know, though what did she mean by the grace of God?

With his new possessions, including the box, Edgar was almost looking forward to the cold time that lay ahead. He wrapped his doona about him like a king, listening to his jug boil, staring at the walls. He never tired of the walls. Staring at them, his thoughts dried up and his body calmed. Then he remembered that he now had a television. Whacko. Things were on the up. Now he had something else to stare at, and when he worked out how to turn it on there'd be no stopping him.

Yema's other great disgruntlement (apart from the theft of his watch, and the injustice of his incarceration — after all, in his country his crime was no crime at all) was the treatment he had received at the hands of the Department in regard to his other item of property. His father's amulet. He showed Edgar a shoebox full of letters and documents in triplicate dealing with or, according to Yema, covering up the issue of the amulet. It was a whitewash.

Edgar sat back and, even though he knew he shouldn't laugh, listened to the funny way Yema told his story.

Firstly, Yema did not want his mother to know he was in gaol, so he wrote to his cousin, Abdullah was his name. He asked for the amulet, a pendant worn around the neck, to be sent to him. Comfort in a time of tribulation. His family had agreed.

Then there had been the problem of postage to a foreign country. Yema hated to think what lies were told to his mother. The amulet was sent, as asked for, to his brother's house in Enmore. Then there was the problem of sending it into the gaol. If it was posted Yema feared that he would never see it. He knew that mail was often thrown in the bin. Finally the brother came all the way from Enmore to visit and brought it with him. As soon as he passed it across the table the officers pounced. The brother was taken away. The other inmates and their visitors, everyone in the room stared at him. It was his worst nightmare. Back in their station the officers cracked open the amulet. Inside they noticed a *brown sticky substance*, which, they said, would have to be analysed down at the lab. Yema lost privileges for six months. That had been two years ago, and despite his protestations, all the letters he had written, he still had no idea what had happened to the amulet.

'They think it drug,' he told Edgar, 'but would anyone be so silly to bring drug into gaol in this way?'

'I dunno,' Edgar said. 'Plenty of silly people round here. What was it?'

'A lock of my father's hair. A pinch of soil from his grave.'

Yema shook the sheaf of papers, all that remained of his quest, before shoving them angrily back in the shoebox, shielding his hot face from Edgar's gaze. If Allah did not charge a soul beyond its capacity, then how much more would he be expected to bear? Edgar wondered why anyone would want to wear those things around their neck. He kept chuckling to himself over that funny word: tribulation.

Another parcel arrived from the woman who called herself his sister. The wrapping had already been opened, but inside it was a pillow, with a crimson pillowslip. He was allowed to keep it. There was another card. It bore the picture of some water lilies floating on a lagoon. Yema awkwardly deciphered the shaky handwriting.

'*Dear Edgar, I hope you can find someone to help you read this message* — That me.'

'Just read.'

'*I have spoken to a lawyer who seems to think there may be grounds to appeal on your fitness to plead. This may take some time, but fingers crossed* —' Yema interrupted himself: 'What means this, this *some* time? Some time? This nothing time.'

'Read.'

'There nothing else. What means this "fingers crossed"?'

'Where's it say my sister?'

'Here,' Yema pointed out the signature, 'Lynne.'

'Lynne.'

He squinted at the name.

'You don't know your own sister?'

Edgar shook his head, and Yema stopped smiling.

'At least she help you.'

'I don't want her fuckin' help. She wanna take me back to that court. That shiny court. I hate it there. They say bad things about me. I won't go. She can fuckorf.'

Edgar trembled with a sudden rage. Yema handed back the card, gazing at his friend for some time.

Years passed, as did the clouds. Edgar became *institutionalised*. In the cold season someone smashed Yema's nose for no reason with a tin of condensed milk swung in a long sock. Perhaps they simply didn't like his nose. Yema was immured in the prison hospital in Sydney. At least he'd be able to see his brother there. His sewing machine, with its stockpile of linen beside it, remained vacant and silent.

Then another man was hunched over the sewing machine like a gold-miner over his pan. Edgar could have sworn it was Mr Ashcroft. Or at least Edgar thought it was the fat manager from the supermarket. Or was it Dungay? He did not speak to Edgar. He did not speak to anyone. Ate his lunch at his machine. Edgar felt sure it was him, unless it was his brainbox playing tricks on him. Edgar grew scared of going to work; of his old conspiracies. Before a cold month had passed Edgar, wheezing through his open mouth, watched another inmate he did not know approach the seated man — who was it? — from behind and, before Edgar had time to do anything other than blink, hit the newcomer, if it was Mr Ashcroft, over the head as hard as possible with a piece of four-by-two from the timber shop. The seated man fell to the floor, dragging the linen with him, and lay there groaning.

'Kid tamperer,' said the second man to Edgar, before sidling away with his wood.

The officers asked Edgar what happened. He didn't know. He didn't know the name of either man. The overseer said that this was not the first time Edgar's proximity to trouble had been noticed. His failure to cooperate. It was in his case notes. Edgar shrugged. 'Trouble foller me.'

An ambulance was summoned to cart the man off to hospital. On the stretcher, looking down at him, Edgar saw that it wasn't Mr Ashcroft at all. Yet it was someone. Edgar had to clean the bloodstain off the floor, which slowed down his quota of flags for the afternoon. He thought he found a piece of brain and flicked it away. The overseer bemoaned the waste of good linen. Again the sewing machine sat idle and silent.

Later Edgar realised that it probably wasn't a piece of someone's brain, but more likely a crumb from the man's lunch.

Seeing him so much alone, Indy and Otto and another friend returned to the buy-up queue to try their luck with him again.

'See you've bought yourself a new telly,' Otto said. 'You must be sewin' plenty of collars and cuffs to save that much.'

Edgar did not reply.

'Be real nice if you loaned your set to Indy for tonight's game.'

Why should he do that? If he did he would never see it again. If he was going to be given another flogging by these blokes, he sighed, then he had better make it worth his while.

'Youse cunts can fuckorf, yer fuckin' rockapes.'

Indy and his pals stared at Edgar's mouth. He wondered, if he could take the words back would it make any difference? Edgar knew his fate was sealed. Perhaps they recalled their last altercation, for they dawdled on their heels and wandered off, looking for the next distraction, which was the yardstick by which they passed the time. Boredom was a great precursor to mischief. Or as Yema had said, evil not attributable to Allah. That afternoon, for instance, when the call came to return to their units for muster, a large group gathered on the top compound, refusing to go inside. Indy and Otto and their cohorts were in the thick of it. Only when the officers assembled in their helmets and vests, did the recalcitrants back down and return to their cells.

No one was surprised when, the next morning, no doors were opened.

Noises in the unit were amplified at night. The rattle of keys on the officers' lanyards; the slamming of cell doors; the fury, or despair, in human voices. The shouting of inmates echoed through the wing. Threats, imprecations; sound for sound's sake. If he stood on his chair and peered through the ventilation grille above his door Edgar sometimes saw small items, usually bungers tied to pieces of cotton, scurry like insects out from under one cell door, around the corner of the dividing wall to the next cell. Sometimes a pencil crept out like the pincer of some predatory animal to work the prize in under the crack. Sometimes men called out to intimidate. But, as Edgar had learned, with two solid iron doors between, nothing could get him in here. Words were just noises. By morning their intent to act had usually dissipated. The day began again.

On nights when there was a big game, every television was tuned to the same channel. There were explosive cheers of elation, or else groans of disgust, when either team scored, or faltered. These cheers and moans, all synchronised so that Edgar sometimes felt they were all together, as one, against a system. Even though he did not understand the rules Edgar enjoyed these games. The combined energy of their roaring at victory, made impotent by the walls, was a sound that gave Edgar a fleeting sense of belonging. The same with their communal silence at defeat. The derision of the victors came later.

If there was a fragile union in this silence, their temporary alliance was even more evident during violent movies, replayed over and over on the video channel. There was nothing more relaxing than lashings of bullet-ridden blood-soaked violence. Every gunshot on the screen wrought a tremendous cheer. There was no perception of irony in this. The bloodier the better. Edgar preferred the football games, but a good massacre seemed to get him pumped up as well as any of them. When the game or movie was over he felt diminished, shrinking into himself like a tortoise under the nose of a dog. The individual threats and cursing started again, as everyone returned to the confines of his cell; the pack turning in on itself, a fox in a trap gnawing its foot off.

It was not unusual for inmates to boast of their crimes. This was their college after all. Edgar had learned how to open locked doors and how to hotwire stolen cars. He knew how to secrete drugs about his person. He knew rather than try to force open a till during a robbery, one simply took the whole till. He knew how to rob a bank and reduce the prospect of a heavy sentence simply by not carrying a weapon. Attitude was as good as a weapon. But he was already doing a heavy sentence. What good was this advice to him? It'll help you when you get out. I'm a old man when I get out. Take it, it's free advice. Advice that he saw was laden with bluff and bravado.

One day the overseer in the textiles shop laid them all off. There was not enough work. Edgar wondered how the demand for flags, for cuffs and collars, for shrouds, could suddenly collapse? He dawdled around the compound catching snippets of conversation here and there, chatting to various colleagues in green. He knew there was nowhere to walk to, other than back again. Nothing was new. For him, as for so many others, a pathway came into being. It was the pacing of caged animals. On the edge of one group he overheard several crooks talking, but one in particular ...

'— the Ampol self-serve at Five Dock, so pissed I took a samurai sword to the bitch at the till. Knew I shouldn't have, but Christ it was fun.'

Edgar looked at the man. Was it Meacham?

'That's the risk they run, ain't it? If they work with cash they've gotta expect to be robbed. Firemen expect flames, don't they?'

Meacham was staring at Edgar. His mouth was moving. Edgar was not entirely sure if the words came from that mouth.

'So I whacked the slut with the flat of it, fuck did she squeal. A shaving nick and she's screaming her head off. Had to give her a thumping to make her shut up. Smack smack smack. "Shutthefuckup lady," I say, "this is a fuckin' armed robbery, whadda you fuckin' expect, good manners?" Nice sword too. Threw it in the river ...'

Laughter.

Edgar circled the group so he could look clearly at the man, but he did not recognise him. Did Meacham know it was him? Edgar could not say.

How did Edgar know it was Meacham? He just knew. The story. Usually these visions came to him in dreams, but here was Meacham, bold as brass, carrying on like the life of the party when he was supposed to be dead as a dodo. Unless it was all tricks in his head. Or unless Meacham had stolen the story. No one else appeared to find Meacham dead as a dodo. They were listening to his every word. Someone was tinkering with his brainbox. Meacham turned to Edgar, if it was Meacham, and said, or seemed to say, 'Mum's the word, eh?' And winked. Edgar said nothing. He went back early to his unit and lay down on his bed, even though he was not tired.

In standing still, time lurched forward. Was it so different on the outside? Work picked up again, they had deadlines to meet. In repetition years passed. Edgar dreamed of dissecting a head of wheat. He dreamed he was in a cave, and in the cave with him was Meacham wrapped in a flag and, in turn, everyone he had ever known. Or else he dreamed that in the cave a dog was waiting.

Sometime after the winter or the summer, Indy appeared in the door of Edgar's cell.

'Howdy, dogman.'

He had with him five others, including Otto, all smiling nastily. When the six had crowded in the cell, blocking his escape, Edgar knew the time had come too late to act. Still he leapt at them with something like a whine of defiance. No time for chitchat. He landed a few solid blows, felt someone's lip burst, but there were too many of them. He held them at bay with his fists and feet and teeth, but too soon they subdued him, sitting on his arms and legs. Their blows were well timed. Indy turned the television on, and Edgar watched in horror as he peeled open a small carton of milk, valuable stuff in anyone's language, and poured it through the vent in the top. The tubes and valves within crackled and spat sparks and popped. The screen went blank. The set fizzed for a while, stinking of burnt milk. Edgar strained in fury against the men holding him down, but they winded him with well-aimed punches to the midriff.

He felt a rib crack. He gasped for air, immobile. They fossicked through his tubs, but Edgar had nothing worth taking. Then Indy took from his pocket an ordinary egg. A speckled chicken's egg, hard-boiled as it turned out, because he cracked it on the wall and began to peel it, flicking bits of shell on the floor. When his egg was peeled he swapped positions with Otto, giving his whole weight to

Edgar's left leg. His muscles cramped with the impossible effort of struggling. Otto also peeled clean his own white, rubbery egg. Then he swapped with another man. Then another, and another. They all had hard-boiled eggs and didn't mind where they threw the shell. Now and then one of them would punch him in the stomach just to keep him quiet. When the sixth egg was peeled they thumped Edgar helpless again and turned him over onto his knees, each limb leaden and numb under the full weight of a man. His pants were reefed down. Edgar strained, but he was weakened now. One of them, Edgar had lost sight of who was who, produced a short length of PVC pipe. He was thumped hard in both kidneys, then the pipe was inserted into his anus and twisted in. He felt the sawn edges of it cut his rectum and gave a muffled cry. Then the first egg was fed into the pipe. Then the second. Then the third. They were tamped down with something that he could not see. Then the remaining eggs were fed, via the orifice of the pipe, into Edgar's sorry arse. Otto chuckled. Edgar could not struggle even if he had the strength. Then the pipe was roughly yanked out, wiped on his back, and the six of them filed out of the cell. Edgar slid to the floor and lay gasping in the shell grit. He did not even register whose room he was in, until he realised it was his own. *Cell*, he thought, it was a cell, never a room. This was where he stared at the walls. Where his tubs were. Sum total of all he was in the world. He saw the dust under the bunk. The smoke of smouldering milk still rose from the television. The act of breathing hurt his ribs. Edgar hoisted himself onto the toilet. He felt like a turtle as the bloody pulp of egg white and yolk fell from him, splashing into the water. He sat there for a long time. When the last had gone he felt a little better. They were only eggs after all, and he had yet to go outside and face them in the yard, but before he did he lay down on the bed and tried to go asleep, go asleep, go asleep.

Later he swept up the eggshells. He emerged briefly to carry the TV out to the officers' station and dumped it on the desk.

'What happened?'

'Milk. Fucked now.'

'You wanna be more careful.'

'I din't do it.'

'Who did?'

Edgar said nothing.

'Do you wanna press charges?'

'I'm sayin' nothing.'

That's what Meacham had said: speak and the stars start to work their dirt against you. He would be expected to take matters into his own hands, to get his own back when no one was looking, or else be seen to be letting them get away with it.

So he said no more and went back to his cell where he stayed like a caveman, studying the grass he saw in the walls.

The sweeper gave him his meals in there. His arse stopped bleeding. He pleaded sick-in-cell and stayed in bed for a week, fostering his delirium in the absence of cartoons. But he knew he could not stay in there forever. He was woken, as usual, by the approaching rattle of keys and when he finally ventured out he saw Yema standing in the wing beside the pool table. Was this another crazy vision? He could not tell. He examined the familiar hook-nose; the eyes darkened more than normal, but he grinned and slapped Edgar on the arm. It appeared he was real. Edgar was happy to see the little man and inspected the way his nose had healed. It had a few extra bumps, but never mind. Edgar happened to know that the cell next to his was vacant, so with a little wheedling they managed to persuade the wing officer to let Yema have it. They were neighbours. Whacko. Yema told him that on days of lockdown Edgar should empty all the water out of the toilet pan, and if he, Yema, did the same, they could communicate quite easily by talking down the toilet. Somehow this filled Edgar with an illicit, mischievous joy, although what they would talk about he did not know.

Work quietened down again. The overseer turned them away. Again they had the days free. Yema was at his wits' end with boredom. They couldn't play tennis; neither of them knew the rules. Yema took him to the clinic where they made an appointment for Edgar to see the dentist. His name and MIN number were written down. They were told that the dentist would need to know Edgar's hepatitis and HIV status, but Edgar did not know what these were. In general, he said, he was pretty fit. The judge had said so. The dentist was a busy man, it would probably take several months.

'Six,' Yema made an educated guess.

They left the clinic and headed for the Education block. These buildings, for Edgar, were also like the familiar dream of strange new rooms in his own house. Simultaneously his horizons broadened and shrank to contain them. It was like the date of his release, burning among the stars. What, he wondered, was behind that fence over there? That, my friend, said Yema, was known as the boneyard, the protection area for dogs and child molesters, not a pretty place. It was but the turn of a key away.

In later weeks Edgar returned to the Education block where not only was he taught the alphabet, but also the combination of letters that spelled his own name. He quickly recalled *Ebgr Ham*. He learned, over time, to write a short sentence that expressed an opinion on a personally relevant topic for which he received a certificate of encouragement. The sentence he wrote was: *The quick brown fox liked*. He couldn't quite reach the end. This was placed on his file, along with his signature, although what the quick brown fox liked remained a mystery. He wrote a CV (with some assistance). It was a great revelation for him to think he had some skills in butchering and might be suited to work in an abattoir. Of the alphabet his favourite letter was S. He also discovered the leatherwork room, where inmates industriously hammered out patterns into sheets of leather. There were various designs of eagles, tigers, bears, dragons, snakes, and skulls. Or else the names of wives, girlfriends, children, motorbikes. Studs were being vigorously thumped, buckles affixed to belts in the tangy odour of glue. The leatherwork teacher asked did he want to join the class? Edgar said he just liked the smell. There were leather satchels, wallets, pouches, all manner of scraps and lacings. The teacher turned away from a bench holding a great wooden mallet. He was helping another inmate punch out the holes for a belt embellished with the design of a snake. There were pictures on the walls of breasty, airbrushed women draped over motorcycles. And suddenly there on the unsupervised desk in front of him was a pair of scissors.

That afternoon again the inmates refused to return to their units. They continued playing tennis. They gathered on the compound, only moving indoors when the squad assembled at the gates in their helmets and riot gear. Two big German shepherds also barked menacingly through the fence. Yema hated dogs. He would rather face ten screws with truncheons than one snarling dog. He moved towards the unit but Indy appeared from nowhere and grabbed him:

'When the time comes, Leb, everyone will have to stay out here. Those who don't will be remembered.'

Yema understood the threat and hurried inside.

Again they locked down the entire gaol and ramped it, cell by cell. They found a bucket full of shivs. When Edgar's turn came he refused to come out so they could ramp unhindered. Four of them, with batons, persuaded him to his knees, then dragged him out like a sack of spuds. Edgar had hidden the scissors inside his mattress which they found in seconds. Consequently he was charged then hauled bodily off to Segregation, struggling all the while, where he spent the next four months.

He looked forward to his meals. Ate with gusto, even the unripe pears. Depending who was on duty, some officers tried to start conversations with him. Sometimes they just opened his door a little and shoved his food in with a boot. Sometimes he answered them: 'Woof.'

Although he hated being manhandled Edgar liked Segro. With all those hours to stare at the walls the days blurred into one. Sometimes, behind the paint, he saw dogs cavorting in the long grass. If he happened to be asleep at the wrong time he could go for a week without seeing daylight. If he did not elect to pace the small yards, which were nothing more than cages, in his allotted hour, then bad luck.

His appointment with the dentist came and went, so he was placed at the bottom of the list again. He received his sixth Christmas card from his sister, which one of the officers read for him. The clinic nurses, who visited regularly, asked if he wanted to be placed on the methadone program.

Whafor? he asked through the bars on his door, I ain't a junkie. That didn't matter, it would help him sleep.

I sleep fine.

The nurses complained to the three-striper, who wrote it in the running sheets, that as they were speaking to Hamilton they could distinctly smell the odour of semen.

'Well, ladies, I'm sad to have to tell you it keeps him quiet, so I'm not about to discourage him in that practice. He can jerk away.'

The chaplain also called to see him with a bundle of *Good News Bibles*. Would Edgar like one? Sure. How was he feeling? Fine. No, he meant how was Edgar *really* feeling? Fine. He wasn't feeling, you know, after all that had happened, under the circumstances, given the past, suicidal? Nup, he felt really fine. After all, your father — Alf wasn't it? — had set the example when Ed was a youngster, hadn't he. All bets were off, weren't they? What's good for the goose. The chaplain could smell the semen too.

'Youse fuckers are all the same, how do yer reckon I should be feelin'?'

The chaplain was pleased to hear that no thoughts of self-harm had crossed the prisoner's mind, do not go gentle and all that.

Edgar barked, 'I'd rather kill some other fucker than kill meself, now once and fer all fuckorf.'

This conversation was also reported; duly noted in the running sheet: *Prisoner made overt threats against other inmates.* I guess the chaplain made a note of it too, somewhere.

Mostly though, the door remained shut.

At the end of five months (an extra one for good measure, and because no cell was available), Edgar was let out into the main compound. He had forgotten the heat of sunlight on his back, the balm of grey rain. It was like a small measure of freedom, until he began to sense over those new days the heightened tension between crims and screws. Things were warming up. Yema was gone. His classification had been reduced, and as a B-classo he had been tipped to a 'better' gaol. That was good. Although he was pleased for Yema, Edgar felt a small nut of bitterness hardening in him. It was softened by the happy news that one of Indy's friends had had his skull fractured after being hit by Hilal Ali with a two-litre bottle of frozen water. Ho hum.

In his old unit, though in a new slot, Indy called out how good it was to see Ed again, and how Yema's running shoes fitted him almost perfectly.

Edgar knew he had to arm up.

He remembered what Yema would have said: think on higher things. He tried to think on his lucky stars. It was hard, but the wall helped.

The inmates from the main population were again refusing to return to their units. It was getting colder; morning fogs. They had a list of gripes which they presented to the Deputy Governor:

1. They didn't like being locked up so early in the afternoon. It was cruel and inhumane.
2. They didn't like being locked up at lunchtime. It was cruel and inhumane.
3. They didn't like the increasing frequency of shutdowns leaving them locked in for days on end. It was cruel.
4. They didn't like the food. It was inhumane.
5. They didn't like the scum in protection receiving privileges which reduced their access to inmate services such as Welfare and Education.
6. They didn't like the pitiful rate of pay they received for a hard day's work. *We demand a pay increase.*
7. They didn't like the fact that they couldn't play real tackle football, only touch.

The Deputy Governor heard their grievances and, in the spirit of political debate, told them to get back to their cells or he would set the dogs on them.

Eventually Edgar did get his teeth. A shiny new set of dentures that enabled him to gnaw through the toughest crusts. They made short work of green pears. His only disappointment was that the rest of him did not live up to the gleam of the new teeth. They also provided him with another means by which to measure time passing. That is, he could now allocate this or that incident to the years before the teeth, or the years after, so that when the riot came, as it inevitably had to, Edgar was able to locate and place it in his own personal chronology. Modest details were released to the media. The riot — or as the inmates called it, *peaceful protest*, to which the screws allegedly overreacted — took place over several days of the autumn after the new teeth. There was a single beech tree amongst the gums on the hill above the gaol and Edgar had watched its golden leaves drift off in the wind like coins. Autumn.

Again, after a period of too many lock-ins, the inmates refused to return to their cells. There were agitators. Was it deliberate provocation? Instead they had gathered on the compound. Some continued to play tennis, despite the repeated demands of the PA system. This had been the pattern over summer, the time Edgar had been in Segro. He saw that Indy and his friends and many others had rugged up in all their clothes, so he too went and fetched his warm, worn jacket. Looked like it was going to be a long night.

It was a pretty half-hearted affair as far as riots go. Most of them were there under sufferance. The screws in the units saw what was brewing and skedaddled before they were swept up in a potential hostage and overtime situation. With the screws out of the way the crims, knowing they would all have to pay the consequences anyway, had a ball. In the yards ten of them picked up the concrete benches and, at a run, hurled them at the steel doors accessing the units. There were cheers when the doors popped off their hinges and flew inward, skidding across the concrete floor.

Inside, screwless, they attacked the officers' stations. The legs were pulled off billiard tables and used to smash the unsmashable perspex windows. What were they doing with billiard tables? In one unit they used the table itself as a battering ram. Once inside the office proper they smashed everything there was to smash. The computers kicked apart, filing cabinets dashed, official documents flung into the air ('Hey, look at this, it says Wilson raped his daughter!'). Edgar's split grin stretched across his face at the wanton destruction. Great sport. Great sport.

Later in the evening (evening outside was such a novelty), the riot squad arrived, all geared up, and proceeded to restore order with their batons and canisters of tear-gas. Clouds of it drifted in the air. They lashed out indiscriminately. Bones cracked. Bodies reeled across the compound, or lay unconscious on the cement. Edgar ran back and forth under the sodium lights along with everyone else. People helping the injured were smashed aside. Dogs savaged their heels. Great sport. Great sport. It was the lowest common denominator. The brutality methodical, just as it was when inmates took brutality on themselves. Edgar was eventually herded into a cell with eighteen others.

'No room, chief.'

'Get in,' came the order, muffled through a gas mask, its demonic eye sockets looking at him like a mad owl. Edgar was almost certain it was Dungay glaring at him through the eyeholes. When they were crammed in, the next order came:

'Kneel.'

There was not enough room for nineteen men to kneel. The ones who were left standing, wedged upright, were knocked flat with batons. Edgar found someone's bloody tooth on the floor. Tear-gas canisters were thrown into locked cells. There were cries of panic as people fought to breathe. Edgar's throat rasped. His eyes burned. His skin crawled with chemicals.

He was blind for four days, while the officers took back control of the gaol and assessed the damage. The inmates lost their billiard tables and their chairs. They lost the concrete benches outside so that there was nothing to sit on but the ground. No one was allowed to play tackle footy. No one got a pay increase. The frequency of lock-ins did not change. Because frozen bottles of water had been used as weapons all unit fridges were removed. Fresh food was consequently removed from the buy-up. Everyone, it must be said, got used to this pretty quickly. It all seemed a bit futile to Edgar, but Edgar had learned that futility was its own reward.

His general memory of it, in the gradual warming of spring, after the new teeth, was one of immense pleasure.

Another Christmas card, plus a rice cooker, arrived from Lynne, the sister. Great, now he had to learn how to cook rice. There had been a bit of a break in correspondence. Mr O'Neil helped him read it. She lived in Melbourne, according to the postmark. They were still working on his appeal, but it was very difficult. Her son was studying law at university and was doing a lot of reading. Money was a struggle. Her health was improving.

Who were *they*? What appeal? Mr O'Neil could not answer him. The fact that Mr O'Neil had cracked a few heads during the riot was generally forgotten between them. (His were the eyes in the owl mask.) Edgar recalled that this nuisance of appealing had something to do with his fitness. Conspiracies or no, all the fitness in the world would be for nought if Indy or someone stuck a shiv in his neck once, twice, twenty times. Any number of ordinary things could happen. They had happened before.

Edgar ground the handle of his toothbrush against the cement floor of his cell until it was as sharp as a tentpeg. He practised jabbing it against the palm of his hand, his throat. Just having it in his cell gave him a sense of security. Yet having it also gave him a sense that he needed it. He wasn't sure who he might need to use it against, there were so many to choose from. Edgar was not diplomatic. Whenever anyone in the compound called out insults to him, he threw them right back, according to the parlance

— if they wanted to fight him, he would fight. He didn't care which group he vilified. They were all coons, slopes, spicks, niggers, wogs, not to mention putrid dogs and gronks, spiders, chats and scum.

'You better pull your head in, son,' one of the officers took him aside. 'It'd be nothing for twenty of 'em to jump you, the shit you give them.'

'What about the shit they give ter me?'

'Are you making a complaint?'

Edgar said nothing.

The officer shrugged. He had performed his duty of care.

In a way this naive fearlessness was why they left Edgar in peace. They remembered what the papers said he had done to his victim. So their taunts rarely went beyond the verbal. Edgar also, truth be told, liked the banter. ('Fuckyez all.')

He was learning how to operate in a social world.

One day, as the members of Edgar's unit were queuing past the trolley to receive their meals from the sweeper, Otto called out:

'Hey, halfwit, lay a egg for me?'

There was laughter along the queue.

'Fuckyer, rockape,' Edgar called back. It was like a cockatoo saying hello.

Otto dropped his easy manner and, in front of everyone, marched across the floor to Edgar. Edgar felt his hackles rise. Zero to ninety degrees was a slow steady ritual. Ninety to one hundred happened in an instant.

'What did you say, gronk?'

'Say, suck my Paddle Pop.'

Edgar had the toothbrush in his hand, eased down from the rubber band around his wrist. Otto brandished his fist, but before he could strike Edgar rammed the toothbrush home, in out, in out, in, up to the bristles in Otto's belly. Otto fell screaming to the floor, a pulse of blood between his fingers. Everyone moved off quickly. No one could reliably say they saw anything. Edgar also moved away and went, without his dinner, but with the music of Otto's squealing in his ears, back to his slot. He knew it was only a matter of time before they figured out whose toothbrush it was.

Alone in his cell Edgar had plenty of time to work himself up into a state of preparedness. He heard the sound of the crime scene being secured; of the others being locked away, the bloodspill cleaned.

Eventually they came and stood in the doorway. Otto had given him up. Edgar would have to go to Segro while they sorted it all out. Would Edgar come quietly?

No, he would not. He was staying here and youse fat maggots could fuckorf as well . . .

Hmm.

'Come on, Ed, we're trying to help here. We've been watching Otto standing over you. We can see it was self-defence, is that the way it was?'

'If yer been watchin' then why din't yer do somethin'?'

When they came into the cell Edgar threw his jug of boiling water over them, clouted the nearest with it. They quickly backed out, one of them holding his nose. There was some similar language to Otto's. One pressed his duress alarm, then called on his radio for assistance with a cell extraction. They slammed the door while they worked out what to do. Edgar sat with his back against the wall, facing the door, so that when they opened the observation flap he was ready, staring them down. The kettle steamed. He might have scissors. They did not know what he had.

When the reinforcements arrived, the door was opened again and a pipper stood there, his underlings behind him.

'Come on, Ed,' said Mr O'Neil reasonably. 'Don't make it any worse for yourself. What if Otto dies?'

'What if?'

'Your life won't be worth shit to his friends. Probably isn't already. We don't want another death in custody here. It's for your own protection. You got plenty to argue in your defence.'

'I don't need protection.'

'Yeah, mate, you do.'

'Protection is fer rockspiders and dorgs. I ain't no dorg.'

'You know we've got to get you out of there, Ed. Otto could have had all sorts of diseases. We got to take a blood sample from you to see if you're all right.'

'You can try,' said Edgar.

'Have it your way. My tea's going cold.'

Mr O'Neil closed the door and Edgar heard him say to the others:

'Call the dogs.'

It was dark and cold outside before he heard the rattle of keys in the lock again. Edgar rose to his feet.

'Is Otto dead?'

'Still early days, but it looks like he's gonna pull through, Ed. Not nearly as bad as it looked. I hear he squealed a bit.'

'He squeal, all right.'

'You'll turn into a caveman if you stay in there.'

Edgar shrugged. 'Plenty to look at.'

'Are you gonna come quietly?'

'Nup. This is too much fun.'

Behind the pipper a German shepherd was dragged into view. The dog's handler jerked its short leash roughly, giving it little lovetaps with his knuckles on the side of its head. The dog curled its lip back and bared its teeth, as it had been trained, in a throaty growl. A part of Edgar admired its teeth.

'Sorry, Ed, you call out when you're ready.'

With that the dog was released into the cell, and the pipper closed the door.

The officers outside later reported how they heard fierce growling from both man and dog — barking, shouting, screaming, howling, yelping, growling. It was impossible to distinguish the sound of man from the sound of dog. For a long time it was ferocious, guttural, and for the screws, highly entertaining.

Then followed a long period of silence.

Inside, the kettle was dashed to the floor. Edgar wrestled for his life with the big dog. Everything happened very fast. Punching or kicking did not seem to hurt it. It had his arm, crunching it in its jaws. Edgar jabbed it in the eye with a finger, then shoved the finger hard up its nostril. It released his arm, but savaged him on every limb before he was able finally to get close enough to get his weight on top of it, his legs around its body, his hands around its throat. They came apart and together again. He had to make sure to keep his legs and lower body close, to avoid the scrabbling paws; to keep his face and upper body away from the fangs. They were on the floor, writhing, until they became partially wedged under the bunk. Edgar tried to cram them both further in. The dog was Dungay. Dungay was the dog. There was no room for the dog to manoeuvre. He used his elbows to prize the front legs apart and away from him. Still his torso was raked from throat to groin. The dog was Meacham. Edgar was Meacham. He wasn't sure how long they remained like this, entangled, struggling, but in the not-so-subtle machinations of instinct it seemed to the man that the dog was now fighting to get away from him. The thrashing of its legs became more frantic. It twisted its head away from him, rather than trying to bite his face. Then he felt its strength begin to wane. The dog was turning to stone. He squeezed his fingers and thumbs even tighter. He had to admire the dog's tenacity, for it was a long time before it was completely still. Edgar did not move. He squeezed his thighs hard around it. Suddenly it seemed that, there under the bunk, the dog was Ivy Cornish. He throttled until his thumbs ached and his fingers locked. They continued to lie there under the bed. Ivy Cornish was the dog. The dog's tongue lolled from the corner of its mouth.

Edgar took the tip of it in his mouth and gnawed it off with the new dentures. He spat it out and when the dog did not react he knew he had won. In their stillness he felt how warm the animal was against his flesh. Ivy warm in his arms. He could smell the chemical perfume of the shampoo in its coat. Her blood was on his face. When he was certain it was dead he slowly disentangled himself, eased out from under the bunk. He found he was aroused.

Outside, the officers listened to the silence, looked askance at each other. It had been going on too long. The dog handler shrugged his shoulders. All along the length of the wing inmates stood on their beds looking out the grilles above their doors. They stared as the door swung open, as it had to, and Edgar slowly emerged with the dog draped limply across both arms. He came out and showed everyone what he had, before flinging the carcass of the dog at their feet. There were muffled cheers, and some laughter from along the wing. The screws stared in disbelief. Then Edgar turned and ambled back into his cell, closing the door behind him. Click.

Inside there was blood all over the floor. Ivy had gone. Edgar breathed. He went to the toilet and, reaching into what he had preserved for just this purpose, began to smear his own shit all over his body, his neck, his ankles, even to his armpits, so as to retain, as it were, when they came for him, a little dignity.

When the officers opened the door for the last time that night Edgar rose from his bunk and stepped out. He was weak and tired now, not as young as he once was. He carried his possessions before him in a single tub. No one tried to touch him. If anything they stepped back and allowed him to pass unobstructed.

FIVE

Edgar sat quietly in the dock. I know, I was there. The shiny railings before him reflected scratches of light. He did not understand what all the beaks were squabbling about, but he tried this time to behave himself; pulled his hands back when he saw his fingers reaching out to fiddle with something. Covered his mouth if he felt the need to belch. Once he stifled a loud yawn when he saw me looking at him. Edgar was called to the stand and answered yes, or no, politely, as far as he was able, when questions were put to him. It had to be explained that he was not on trial for hurting Otto. Otto had declined to press charges. This was a separate matter. He listened with all his might. He said it would help him if we could keep our questions short and simple. No, he did not have a full recollection of the original trial, only of being immensely tired. That was why he didn't like court. And because they said bad things about him which weren't true. Lynne had flown up again and sat at the back of the gallery smiling encouragement to him. She was wearing smart, new clothes, but looked like a scarecrow now, to Edgar.

In the intervening years she had undergone chemotherapy. Her hair was still growing back in soft tufts beneath a silk scarf. I had steeled myself against this vision that was not my mother. I'd chosen not to delve into the privacy of her illness, and had lost myself in study and work, symptoms, I think now, of a breaking heart. I am not good with medical nomenclature.

I had just completed my Articles and was a bright young solicitor with Pennington, Arnold and Gorse. I had a future. I had Emily who, I hoped, would one day become my fiancée. We went dancing and hiking and swimming at the beach; we enjoyed movies and music and restaurants. This was a life away from my mother's disease, and the secret, weird uncle from her past. Each weekend now, as she pored over complicated legal judgements, and rang me with obscure questions, I told myself I would have a much better time if I only kept my nose out of her business. But I could not stay out of it.

My mother could not manage more than a rudimentary understanding of the legal technicalities which impinged upon her brother's circumstances. Yet she had become determined to argue the injustice of his case. So I could not say no. It was either that or close myself up to her like a clam. This was the last good thing she had set herself to do. As she said, she had treated her own parents abominably by running away; this was some kind of gesture of atonement.

So the time came when I said to Emily one weekend that we could not go dancing as we had planned, nor spend all Saturday in bed, as was sometimes our custom. I took the files and papers into my study and closed the door to wrestle, as Emily so kindly put it, with my doppelgänger.

I was now assisting Mr Pennington, who had agreed to take the case *pro bono*. I did not tell my mother that Pennington had once taken a considerable fee to defend extradition proceedings against a Lebanese drug baron and then not even bothered to turn up in court.

The further I had read into Edgar's case, the more I became disturbed. There was no doubt in my mind he'd been stitched up by sloppy investigative work, as well as sloppy jurisprudence. However, as Pennington pointed out, we were not at this stage appealing the conviction.

'His guilt is neither here nor there, Tony, all we are attempting to do is free him from custody. We are exploiting a technicality, when perhaps the morally correct thing to do would be to leave him where he is.'

'Or not.'

'Or not,' he agreed. 'Morality is largely irrelevant.'

When I reported to Mum that Pennington had agreed to take the case, and that she should fly up to meet him, she hissed a sibilant 'Yes!' through the phone.

For the police at the time, the arrest of Edgar had been a quick result. Good work, lads. Good PR. As regards his fitness to plead, one of the stumbling blocks in our grounds to reventilate the matter, apart from the ancient precedent of *R v Dyson* (1831) — the deaf woman made mute by the visitation of God — was the case of *R v Chad*. As a young lawyer I was quickly learning to fathom the depths to which a man can sink. The Chad story was too bizarre to be concocted. I did not wish to relate it to my mother — but she found out for herself, looking through microfiche archives of old newspapers. As Pennington said, the subjectivity of truth was its only usefulness.

Young Chad had had a record of petty theft, and a string of other misdemeanours accompanied by short sentences. He was a thickheaded boy with no one to tell him what to do. One day in 1983 he killed a girl — or, as he claimed (as Edgar also claimed), he found the body of a girl. No one believed him, of course. What they believed was the physical evidence. Which said: That he had intercourse with the girl and tied a rope around her; that he anchored it to a tree and threw her body into a river. (The river as crime scene was another importunate coincidence.) That he returned the next night and fished her out and did the same. That, on the third night he returned and did the same. That, on the fourth night he returned with intent to do the same, only to be caught, as it were, on the job, when the police jumped out of the bushes.

Chad was sentenced as a 'forensic patient' and held at Touringa Hospital in the secure ward. That is, he was *a person detained in a hospital, prison or other place* pursuant to an order under both the *Mental Health (Criminal Procedure) Act 1990*, and Section 7(4) of the *Criminal Appeal Act 1912*.

'Speak English!' my mother snapped 'What does all that gobbledegook mean?'

Well — if it had not been for the political push to close down many of the psychiatric and mental health facilities in the community, people like Chad, and Edgar for that matter, would have had somewhere to live, some prospect of treatment. Instead they had lived out on the street. Where the political climate then also worked a similar weather against them.

Next, Chad escaped from the hospital, having attacked and bound with gaffer tape three of the staff on night duty. He was out in the community for five days, though he made no attempt to disguise or conceal himself. After that, there was nowhere else to keep him other than in gaol.

You can imagine, Mr Pennington explained to my mother over coffee in his office, how popular that crime would make him in prison.

'Your brother's record of causing trouble whilst in custody would be regarded as too close a similarity to Chad's case for the authorities to risk transferring him out of custody.'

'But he shouldn't be there to begin with.'

'That's what we'll be arguing,' Mr Pennington agreed, 'but whatever the outcome of that course of action, it is still a possibility that your brother may be guilty. There was a similar debate about whether Chad was fit to stand trial: whether he was mad or not at the time of the offence, something had to be done with him. He is now regarded as an ordinary man.'

'Chad is not my brother.'

'Chad is serving thirty-five years. Your brother is looking good by comparison. Does that alter your thinking at all?'

'No.'

My mother adjusted the scarf on her head. She smelled of chemicals.

'To be blunt, Mrs Tindale, what I don't understand is why you seem intent on martyring yourself.'

'I'm not a martyr, Mr Pennington. I'm just doing what I believe is right. I ran away from Edgar once and left him in that dreary, godforsaken place. I didn't even help when he was being born. All my life I have thought only of myself, although I've often wondered how he survived in the midst of all that awfulness. Perhaps it's worse for a girl. I don't want to turn my back on him again.'

'Could you live with yourself if your brother were to re-offend?'

'I don't believe he has committed an offence in the first place.'

'In that case, Tony,' Pennington turned to me, 'you had better arrange a meeting with Mr Hamilton.'

After the cold months of Segro, Edgar was escorted (he wasn't frogmarched or dragged or manhandled in any way) down to the boneyard. No one had horns or cloven hoofs. They were just a variation of the same. Just as many tattoos. He recognised plenty of blokes from the Main who had bailed for one reason or another, unable to handle the rough and tumble any more. Meacham wasn't there.

Mr O'Neil told Edgar that Otto would not die.

'Pity,' said Edgar.

Otto was in Long Bay Hospital after some surgery to repair a perforated bowel. There were no witnesses to the incident, so there was nothing to charge Edgar with — everyone knew that the life of a dog wasn't worth diddly. Otto had slipped on the toothbrush. What it did mean, however, was that Edgar would be unable to return to the Main. Indy and all his friends would be out to even the score.

Edgar, as they say, still had more gaol in him.

'I ain't signing on Protection.'

'You've got no choice, Ed. We're not letting you back out there with them.'

'I can protect meself.'

'That's the trouble, Ed. Indy and his mates might need protecting from you.'

The Protection Unit was full to overcrowding. It was another type of pressure cooker. Everyone wanted to be protected from something. Young lads had to be protected from predators. The lifers had to be protected from their own notoriety. Society had to be protected from the likes of them. Edgar was asked if he was likely to slash-up? If he was, they would place him in an observation cell where the light bulb burned all night.

No, he said again, he would rather knock someone else than kill himself.

'Sounds like you don't need any counselling then.'

Edgar was placed in a two-out cell that he was to share with a grey-haired, silver-bearded older man, although Edgar, with his own scrappy bits of beard, did not know how old he himself might look.

'Here you go, Fletch,' said the officer, opening the door and introducing them, 'you can convert the heathen dogman.'

The cell was identical to all the others Edgar had seen, except that it contained two bunks. The man was already ensconced on the bottom one, tucked under a floral doona. He was not happy.

'Chief,' he called, getting awkwardly to his feet, 'chief, you've got to find me a one-out.'

'They're all taken.'

'I can't share with anyone else.'

'Bad luck.'

The door was closed. Click.

There was a little mauve curtain hanging over the window. Pictures on the walls, not of naked girls, but of rivers, trees, country landscapes. There were books. Edgar counted ten, which was the maximum allowable limit. And — Edgar's spirits soared — Fletcher had a television. He looked at the man he was now to spend eighteen hours a day with for the foreseeable future. His ears sprouted tufts of white fur. Did Edgar know him? He could not say. At least he did not look like Meacham. Edgar threw his tub into the corner, then he held out his hand.

'G'day ter yer too, fellah.'

The old man, resigned to his entrapment, responded:

'Yes. I suppose. Hail, young fellow.'

And they shook.

It was harder for Fletcher than it was for Edgar. Edgar farted. A lot. He chose odd, if rare, times to shower. He picked his toenails and flicked the parings about the floor. He urinated loudly in the toilet. He picked his nose with every finger. He masturbated on the top bunk — as they say in the slot, every night he had a kill. His favourite television shows were cartoons.

('Have you no consideration for anyone?' Fletcher cried out, once they had got to know one another. Fletcher must have put up with a lot.

'Eh? What's that big word? — Consider-*what*? Do you ever have that for me?')

They were quickly getting along like an old married couple.

One day a week, they had access to the Education block and Fletcher insisted that Edgar go there, that he should try to learn to read and write.

'I can write me name,' said Edgar defensively. 'I got a certificate.'

But when Fletcher put him to the test he found that Edgar mixed up his b's and p's and d's and q's. He signed his name *Ebgr Ham* with a tail of ink meandering to the end of the page.

'Just like a doctor,' said Fletcher.

Edgar looked forward to Wednesdays, and Fletcher, who did not attend Education, looked forward to a brief respite from Edgar's company. Both were extremely cranky if Education was thwarted for any reason. In time Edgar wrote a letter to his friend Yema and told him about the weather, but he did not know where Yema was any more. Fletcher worked on the ground maintenance gang, which cut the grass around the sterile zone. He complained constantly that the plovers swooped him when he pushed his mower too close to the camera poles, but Edgar envied him, at least he was outdoors.

Each evening Fletcher kneeled at his bunk and covered his face with his hands, mouthing soft words to himself. Once Edgar had the curiosity to ask him:

'What yer doin'?'

'I'm praying.'

Edgar laughed. They each thought the other was mad. Fletcher did not ask Edgar what he was in for. Nor did Edgar ask what was Fletcher's crime, although Fletcher delighted in telling Edgar which other inmates were in for chopping up people and stuffing them in suitcases (of whom there was no apparent shortage). It was enough to know the length of the sentence. That gave a hint. Fletcher was doing ten on the bottom with sixteen on the top. He'd done nearly eight already so he was looking forward to his release on parole in two years' time. He'd been a good boy, a model prisoner. It was the screws who let slip to Edgar, in tones of tedious revulsion, that his cellmate was in for taking photographs of things he shouldn't have been photographing. Sick photos. Of children whom he had drugged. A sex pest. Struggling with his understanding of this, Edgar had no choice but to live with it. One night he woke up with a start. Fletcher was standing no more than a foot away, staring at him.

'Do I know you?' Fletcher asked.

Edgar growled and rolled over. One thing gaol had taught him was that nausea was relative. He wondered if he should kill Fletcher in the night. He did not think a kiddie tamperer would present as much of a problem as the German shepherd. In the end he decided not to, as they would probably find someone just as bad to stick in with him, one of the lifers with nothing to lose; someone without a television. Besides, Fletcher had begun to read to him from his ten books, which he would change every now and then at the gaol library. There were many writers, Fletcher said, many modern masters who had tried to describe the prison experience. Many, many, going back to the less modern. Even that slippery penologist Foucault had had some interesting insights. Of course they had romanticised it terribly. Crime and punishment, sin and redemption, these were perennial themes of human experience. If one thought about it, one could think oneself out of this place. The life of the unshackled spirit rose above confinement. Sometimes, he said, he felt like Raskolnikov, but none of them, none of these brilliant minds, knew what he knew. None of them had the finely illuminated perception that he possessed in the light of all this knowledge.

'Huh?' Edgar often said.

Fletcher had been a Catholic priest.

'You talk too much.'

He liked listening to the stories, but there were too many tricks in words. He liked the sound of Fletcher's voice, but if truth be known he preferred the cartoons.

This did not stop Fletcher, who also liked the sound of his own voice, and gave running commentary on the books he read from. He pontificated on an endless range of subjects. Sometimes Edgar would wake in the night and Fletcher would be standing at the window whispering to himself. He theorised, pacing in front of Edgar, who gazed dully at the Roadrunner, or Rugrats, or Angela Anaconda. Fletcher went on about his fellow inmates whom he considered, unlike him, to be the dregs of humanity.

'I thought you was the dregs of that,' said Edgar.

It was a commercial break. Fletcher looked taken aback that Edgar had spoken.

'What? Because I'm here in Protection?'

'Because yer a spider. You wouldn't stand a snowflake's out there.'

'And what are you?'

'I like dregs.'

Fletcher was silent, and then the cartoons started again, the coyote falling to his death beneath an anvil, only to bounce back again. When this claimed Edgar's attention, Fletcher laughed out loud.

One night, after Edgar had noisily finished his ablutions, Fletcher, lying with his face to the wall, said:

'This is Hell. I'm in Hell.' It was like a realisation. 'It's Camus.'

'It sure ain't no picnic,' said Edgar, flushing the boghole.

Suddenly, climbing up to his bunk, he was a boy again. He heard his voice utter the father's phrase. The same lilt and intonation to the words. They felt like stones in his mouth. His mind was suddenly filled with the father. *Never marry a woman, my lad, unless yer can stand ter watch 'er chokin' with a bit of pepper on 'er tonsil*. He lay staring at the ceiling, thinking of Alf. He could hear the faint whistle over the top of his father's teeth as he worked, smell the boots he kicked into the corner of the kitchen. *Fetch my tea. Pass the salt*. He could smell his father's breath, see the hairs on the back of his hands. He knew the space between the freckles on his arms. Edgar was aware that Alf was not present in the cell, but he knew every shape the hand made.

Slowly he realised that Fletcher was still talking.

'Didn't you hear a word I said?'

'What word?'

'You weren't listening?'

'You talk too much.'

Fletcher laughed.

'Ed, you're the perfect confessor. You listen, but you don't hear. And you don't judge.'

'I ain't no judge. It were a judge put me here.'

'Me too, Ed, me too.'

Fletcher resumed his pacing.

So while Edgar thought of the father, heard, smelt, felt the bristles of his jowls — and in time thought of his mother, and in time, the silky — Fletcher, meanwhile, revelled in the confession of his crimes, made to the waxy cavity of Edgar's deafness. What he had taken his photographs of, the types of camera he had used, what he was doing while he took them. He elaborated what had tempted him in the first place: a child's eyes, a pout, her plaits, the gullibility of the mother. He was a lover of children, not some clichéd abuser. Edgar did not listen. He drifted in and out of sleep. He heard the vocal drone, but he was standing in the grass with the father. There were dogs. He wondered where were the grassdogs now? Not here, but out in the long grass — in the paddocks which swayed in the paint on the walls.

Fletcher wanted to know what was Edgar thinking about? Was he listening? But Edgar, as according to Meacham, guarded his dreams. Fletcher was sordid. Or was it Edgar's dreams that were bestial? Something in Fletcher's tone filtered through to Edgar. It was the grandstander absorbed with his own voice, rather than — another big mouthful that Fletcher spat derisively — the penitence of the sinner.

Edgar remained, according to the precedent, mute by the visitation of God.

And deaf. He barely listened. He drifted to the paddocks with the father, traipsing through crops of wheat or lupins, a dog swimming in the grass, the great wide sky overhead. He did not hear Fletcher's mantra: 'If only they knew, if only they knew.' He did not register Fletcher's allusion to the fuss made over this child or that child or one girl missing in particular. Edgar saw his own hand pushing open the door of the shearing shed. They always made such a fuss when a girl went missing. What sort of slutty mothers were they, to go off and leave their daughters in his charge? Dusty sunlight falling from the nailholes in the roof. They were just exploiting him for free babysitting. One of them had actually said to him: 'After you've finished with her you can come and do it to me.' Sometimes Edgar snored. He breathed the smell of lanolin.

He did not understand why Fletcher quizzed him at the end of each evening's instalment, asking how much Edgar had understood of his sorry purgation.

'What are you thinking about?'

'Eh? Nothin'.'

'Didn't you understand a word I said?'

'You yabber too much.'

'You're incredible.'

'It don't matter if I listen or not, you'd still be yabberin'.'

According to Fletcher, God was listening to him through the holy ears of the idiot savant.

Edgar did not listen to the dreamy admission to the accidental overdose of Rohypnol. Nor the sudden young body that had to be disposed of after Fletcher had finished his business. His photography.

'I mean, Ed, what would you do?'

No reply. Edgar's reverie resumed. The peppercorn tree bowing over the shed. Fletcher's words drifted against the ceiling. He went on about the fuss that infected the entire district where he was once parish priest after being transferred from Queensland. Edgar did not understand the options that had paraded themselves through Fletcher's panicky mind. None of them had ever died before. They had all liked him. He had tortured himself over whether to make a full confession to police. Perhaps plea-bargain for manslaughter. It would have eased his conscience. But conscience was a social construct; it was a tool of oppression, and he had risen above dogma. Besides, he had his good works to perform. Edgar dreamed of dogma. Of scrawling in the dust with a stick. Instead, when Fletcher was caught, he only admitted to the photographs they could identify, which, even the jury admitted, could have been of anyone — while they carried on the search for someone else miles away. Edgar could smell pepper. They dragged the river twice. Hope dried up. Just another unsolved case. A local suicide deflated the passion for the search. Handy red herring, that. Most of Fletcher's victims were in Queensland so the scent was now well and truly cold. They would never find her. While he was here, right under their noses serving time for something altogether different. Almost innocuous.

Justice was not the province of the Church, as salvation was not the domain of the courts. A shame really, such a pretty face.

Edgar drifted through the grass. Heard the different voices of the dogs. He did not comprehend the big words Fletcher used in his boasting, and did not try to. The sound of his voice was lulling, as it went on, night after night, hypnotically. Edgar slept. The scarecrow of the mother came and cooked scones in the corner of the cell. He dreamed of her searching in the grass for the flour. So he did not understand what Fletcher muttered. Some caves in a range of hills. They had no name. They weren't even on the official maps. No one knew they were there. Even the blacks had forgotten they had performed initiation rituals there. They were just hills without names and were known only by the small town at their base. Edgar looked up, the horizon swayed with grass — a small nowhere town — at the blue silhouette — called 'the Rock'. The search never even got close —

Here, lying as he always did on the top bunk, Edgar's ears twitched. He fell suddenly back into his body. Listening. Suddenly he knew where he had seen Fletcher before. Without a beard. Not in a dream with Meacham.

It was at the Rock that Fletcher disposed of the remains, buried in an anonymous cave, miles from the site of the search. They'd never find her. Poor little Sophie. Such a pretty face. If only they knew. Was Ed awake? Huh? Did he understand a word that Fletcher was saying to him? Nuh. Did he remember the girl's name for instance?

'Shut up, I'm tryin' ter sleep.'

Edgar grumbled and rolled over, wide-awake, for when he thought about it he did remember the girl's name. Sophie T. And other details besides. Rohypnol. The colour of her underwear. Details that Fletcher had happily revealed.

Edgar kept these details to himself.

He asked if Fletcher remembered a TV show called *Huckleberry Hound*?

I don't believe Edgar knew he had a cause, which I guess is pretty much the point, while for my mother time was running out. Trucks came and went, in and out of the big gates. Inmates arrived and disappeared overnight. The prison population was in constant transit. Only Edgar seemed stuck fast.

The following summer, after Christmas, Edgar was informed he was to have a visitor. But the gaol was locked down, so the visitor was told to return the following week. Edgar did not know who to expect, but when he entered the visiting section, locked in a pair of white overalls that were zipped up the back and secured at his neck, there, perched on a chair bolted to the floor, was the mother. Quickly he realised it could not be her. The mother was dead as a dodo. It must be the sister. He faintly recalled her sitting in the courtroom during his trial. And at the mother's funeral. Yes. He definitely recognised her. But did that recognition go deeper? She was much older. Today she wore an orange cardigan. He could smell perfume.

'Hello, Edgar,' she said, standing up. Her hand was small and cool.

'Lynne?' he tried the name, a stone in his mouth.

I rose beside her and shook my uncle's hand. I was almost his height. His hand was cold and strong. I introduced myself but he did not remember me. I tried not to look at his lip.

They exchanged some pleasantries — the drive out to the gaol, the accommodation she had found in town. The unfortunate delay. He thanked her for her Christmas cards. He kept them in his tub. And for the doona. And the rice cooker. I did not know she had been sending him Christmas cards. He explained, in brief, about the television. I stole glances at the way his tongue worked in his mouth. *How* had she talked me into this? *How* could she say *but for the grace of God*? The only resemblance I could see was the colour of our eyes.

This was no time for small talk. Why had she not come sooner? he asked, and that was something I also wanted to know.

Because she had been sick. She had been sick and for a long time she had believed her husband who thought that Edgar was guilty.

I wanted to interrupt, to get the business underway, but my uncle had other ideas. He wanted some answers to questions he could barely conceive of: When? Who? Why? She told him she had run away from home, the first time when she was thirteen. Edgar was a baby. She hated the farm. The desolate tedium and the emptiness. The sky's oppression, and the poverty of the dust. She did not want to be reminded of her father and his despair, the constant bickering and broken crockery. Their father, from whom she had stolen money and fled.

That was all she was prepared to tell him of the past, for which I was grateful. I was in a young man's denial about the status of his parents' relationships. Only to find there was a whole history of dysfunction. I did not wish to know about her past. The here and now was where I thrived. Emily's kisses were still fresh on me from that morning.

Why had he never known he had a sister?

Because, she presumed in a rather wooden way, they hated her. When she had run away for the last time, perhaps a year after they had come home with the new baby, she had tried to burn their house down. She had set petrol-soaked rags alight in the laundry. The father had caught her and beaten her. He had threatened to burn all her things if she ran away again. She felt that life had not been kind to her, so why should she be kind? To stay would have been to surrender to the cruelty of the world. So she had struggled through adolescence without help from anybody. She was not proud of her actions in the past. She was in rebellion against fate and the utter desolation she saw around her.

This was the worst conversation I can remember overhearing.

'You saw me when I were a nipper?'

'Yes.'

'Maybe you left because I scared you away?'

'No, Edgar. I used to sing to you until they told me to shut up and let you sleep.'

'Sing?'

There was a moment when she might have broken — an unbearable moment borne by all, before my mother changed the subject. I raised my hand to my own shaved and perfect lip; the one Emily loves to behold and kiss.

Emily, whose belly is already achieving a three-month tautness, like a drumskin over the burgeoning progeny we are adding to the world. The child who may well look like my uncle. I made a mental note to suggest a prompt amniocentesis.

Lynne was surprised that Edgar had not been turned against her. She had come prepared to defend herself. Edgar turned his palms up. He didn't know. He was not clever enough to understand these things. Despair and poverty were not what he remembered. The old folks liked their grog, he knew that. Why had she come now? She began to explain about her cancer, her guilt, but faltered.

This is where I stepped in:

'Because, Edgar, there's going to be an appeal. I've been looking into your case and there are many legal technicalities yet to be sorted through, but apparently the judge erred in not allowing a second inquiry to determine whether you were fit to stand trial.'

'It means,' said Lynne, 'that if it's successful, you might be granted clemency.'

'Let's not jump the gun.'

'But I got seven years to go. More for Otto. I'm a bad boy.'

'Well, Edgar, the fact is that if you weren't fit to stand trial you shouldn't be here.'

Edgar stared at us for a moment. It was impossible to read his feelings.

'Are yer come ter laugh at me?' he demanded.

'No, no, Edgar,' I said. 'It's not like that. If what you said to Maureen Henry is true, then I'm here to say I want to help you.'

'What I said?'

'That you found Meacham's body.'

'That true.'

'That you knew him.'

'Sort of. Meacham said they'll try and whittle you down. We's all missing something. His fingers, the tripod's leg, me teeth, Lynne's hair. I wonder what you's missin', Tony?'

I tried to divert attention away from this specific query.

'It's a complicated area of law. We need the guidance of my boss, Mr Pennington. That is, Edgar, if you want to be helped.'

'If yer reckon I do, Tony, then yeah, I need yer help.'

'Then I'll help.'

My mother gripped her brother's hands. An announcement came over the loudspeakers. Lynne looked around the visiting section. The bars on the windows, the cameras behind their dark domes in the ceiling. So too did Edgar. So did I. It was new to us all.

They continued to talk for another half an hour. Edgar made her a brew in a styrofoam cup. She had brought him lollies. He stuffed a handful into his mouth, then, so as not to appear greedy, offered us some. We declined. She pulled out some photographs of me as a child. There was nothing under the age of two. And was that her little Jack Russell terrier in the background? Yes, yes, it was. She slipped the photos back into her handbag. How he wished he could have rummaged amongst all the little things she kept in that bag. She took out some lip salve and applied it. She saw him watching her, then gave it to him.

'It must be terrible for you here.'

'It ain't too bad. Yer get used to it.'

'I had to sell the house at Uranquinty. There wasn't much standing. Dungay bought it.'

Edgar shrugged.

'What's a house?'

He wondered about the wallaby hide he had left over the window in the lounge room, which must have gone straight to the tip in the first load.

I went through the correct procedure to book a legal visit in a month's time. I would need to interview him again. When we left we shook hands again formally. He thanked us for coming, as if it had been a pleasant afternoon.

'See you in court, Edgar,' she said.

'I hope I won't have to go to court again. I feeled real bad there.'

'I know,' she said, 'it's no picnic.'

His grimace was a smile. Had he understood anything I'd said? He clutched the lip salve in his hand.

On the way back inside, the screws confiscated his lollies. Food had to be consumed within the visiting section. No consumables could be brought back into the gaol. If he wanted lollies he could purchase them on the buy-up like everybody else. They made him strip, then dress again in his prison greens.

Back in their cell Fletcher wanted to know all about Edgar's visitor, but Edgar would not tell him. He feigned forgetfulness, which infuriated Fletcher beyond temperance. Edgar felt that if he spoke he would blubber, his heart was raw and breaking and blossoming all at once. There were too many emotions at work in him. Fletcher changed tactics. He tried to draw Edgar into his conspiracy.

'Look what I found, Ed, out in the sterile zone, I found them when I was mowing. I'm getting darned sick of them swooping me. How about we boil them up in your jug and add them to our dinner?'

In his hand Fletcher held out three speckled plover's eggs, the colour of stones. Edgar stared at them, then he snatched them out of Fletcher's hand and flung them against the wall.

Legal papers soon arrived. They burned with menace on the desk. Fletcher refused to read them for him. He was still cranky about the eggs.

More than anything Edgar was terrified of the prospect of freedom. Where would he live? What would he do? Edgar knew of men who had mutilated themselves so as to avoid being released. Fletcher, relenting, told him he was mad to even think about such things.

'*A thousand years in thy sight are but as yesterday when it is Past.*'

'You said this was Hell.'

'Did I? Well, yes, there's that, but once it's over, liberty, that sweetest fruit . . . '

They had grown used to each other. They were necessary torment. Edgar looked at Fletcher and knew that the priest had no idea what was going on in his mind. He was thinking more and more that he should kill Fletcher while he slept. He could tip a jug of boiling water over him, and stab him to death with a Biro. It might not kill him outright, but it would sure be fun. Would a man who was not fit to stand trial think such thoughts? Was this what they meant by rehabilitation? Being unfit to plead and knowing he was unfit to plead were two different things. If he was unfit to plead at the time of his trial, all those years ago, what was he now? And if he now knew that he was unfit, was that knowledge he should rightly keep to himself?

So he did. He kept Meacham's silence. Before the cold and sleet began again to dance about the compound, and frost began to ice the weeds, the legal papers had burst into flower and the appeal hearing was announced. Fletcher soured at the prospect that Edgar might even be released before him. It was fine for him to preach about freedom, but he resented that Edgar might be favoured sooner than he — an educated man, especially considering Edgar's intellect.

'You're not ready for society, Ed. You wouldn't cope.'

Edgar knew he had read the legal papers. He stopped reading aloud from his ten books. He stopped embellishing his nightly confessions. He held his words back as if withholding some reward of companionship.

'And society's not ready for you.'

'Do yer think I fuckin' care about that sick shit yer get orf on?' Edgar yelled suddenly.

There was a pause. The shower dripped.

'Ed,' said Fletcher, shocked, 'after all I've done for you.'

'Fuckyer, Father priest.'

'You threw my eggs at the wall.'

Edgar was suddenly racked with anger. Fury quickly filled their too-small confines. The lowest common denominator. He seized Fletcher by the hair and tossed him out of the bottom bunk onto the floor. The older man screamed.

'Time fer a change, priest, I reckon,' he snarled, claiming the bed for himself. He tossed Fletcher's bedclothes onto the floor, then remade his own bed there. Fletcher stood cowering in the shower cubicle.

'But that's my bed, Ed. I can't sleep up there.'

'So don't sleep.'

Edgar was so sickened by Fletcher's wheedling fear that he turned the shower on and soaked him to the skin.

'Don't hurt me.'

Edgar switched the television on and picked the set up and held it above his head. This is easy, he thought. Killing is easy. They stared at each other. The water cascading over Fletcher's face to the pool at his feet. Edgar with the TV blaring above his head. Neither of them was certain how long the lead was.

There was a word they used in the Main to describe people like Fletcher, and Edgar used it now. He said:

'Putrid.'

Then he spun around and tossed the television back on the bench, where it fizzed and popped and shit itself and went out. Fletcher quickly jumped out of the water. Turned off the taps.

'You're mad,' said Fletcher, 'you're an imbecile, you're not fit to be free, you don't know anything.'

'I know how the hanging bit fell off Hanging Rock.'

'What?'

'I know where you dump Sophie.' Edgar stared at him.

Whatever else Fletcher thought remained unspoken.

Edgar asked the unit barber to give him a haircut. He was soothed by the coolness of the man's fingers against his neck, folding his ears aside. The hum of shears. His caveman curls fell to the floor. He felt the coolness of the air on his neck. His life taking on new proportions.

'I look real good,' Edgar said, examining his reflection in the burnished metal.

'No worries, Ed, it's not fuckin' brain surgery.'

'Thanks. I don't need brain surgery.'

* * *

'All stand.'

Edgar stood. I had made several visits to coach him on court protocol and etiquette, and also to try and make some sense of his story.

Now the judge had returned after the lunch adjournment, and legal argument resumed. The gallery had been closed to the public. Edgar sat up straight. The perfunctory nature of the Crown case was noted. The police had not investigated the possibility that a knife other than Edgar's may have been the murder weapon. Or indeed that Edgar's story might have been true.

('Remember, Tony,' said Pennington, 'innocence is beside the point.')

Edgar shuffled in the dock. Submissions were made that the original trial judge, who had passed away in the intervening years, had expressly ignored the *good faith* in which persistent requests for a second fitness hearing had been made. That had been, your Honour, because the matter of fitness or unfitness clearly fell beyond the adversarial parameters of a criminal trial. (Pennington cited legal precedents for this statement.) A position with which we disagree.

Yes, yes, thank you, Mr Pennington.

The judge then tried to define what the Law meant by *good faith*.

Pennington went on. Psychological testing, dredged from the court records, had placed Mr Hamilton's communication skills at the approximate age of six and a half. Yet the trial judge had viewed him as deliberately mendacious. Further testing described Edgar as moderately intellectually disabled, hence his ability to live independently. His living skills were assessed as being commensurate with an age of about nine years and five months.

Back and forth the debate rallied. These various assessments discounted the defence of insanity according to the McNaughton Rules of 1843: Mr Hamilton clearly did not have a disease of the mind.

However the court would be reminded by Mr Pennington that at the time of his arrest Mr Hamilton had been living like a dog — he had even been found on all fours — is that the behaviour of someone who understands the nature and quality of their behaviour?

To each their own, Mr Pennington.

The Crown intervened: What were his living skills like now after all this time in gaol?

That is a hypothetical slur on the reputation of the

Department, whose charter is to return people to society *no worse* than when they were incarcerated.

And how, pray tell, is that determined? Pennington wondered.

This is neither the time nor forum to discuss such issues, my learned friend.

'I can write me name,' Edgar piped up, but was silenced by a look from our bench.

'Are you currently taking medication, Mr Hamilton?'

'No fear. I don't touch drugs.'

'Have you been attending educational programs whilst in gaol?'

'Yep.'

I produced as evidence certificates for reading and writing: *The quick brown fox liked Ebgr Ham.* His work record impressed the judge.

'I see you are able to write a coherent sentence.'

'Yep. I can write a letter. I got a CV.'

'That's good, Mr Hamilton. Very commendable.'

Mr Callow, representing the Crown, was perplexed as to why, after all this time, we had engaged a person of the stature of Mr Pennington to pursue the matter with such vigour? Mr Pennington's reply, as the rest of his performance, was impeccable: injustice anywhere was intolerable in a humane society. And I saw my balls sink to the bottom of his pocket.

The discussion continued: His living skills were all very well, but the level at which he functioned in the community had no bearing on how he functioned in court. Unfitness was clearly the only reasonable conclusion that could now, in retrospect, be made. And if he had been unfit at the time of the crime, then where, pray tell, was the mens rea? In that event, if the court sees fit to find it so, Mr Hamilton should have been, and should now be regarded as a forensic patient. In which case most forensic patients might expect to be placed on a limiting term, so as to ascertain whether a reduced sentence is warranted. Indeed, given the time already served, a forensic patient charged with offences of a similar gravity as Mr Hamilton's would have been discharged before now, pending fresh psychological assessment to determine his social adaptability, and indeed, any potential danger he may pose to the community. He would, at the least, have received psychological counselling; appropriate medication. Presumably there is no evidence of these activities because they did not happen. In any event his security classification would have been reduced by now — what was he still doing in maximum security?

The court ordered that such an assessment be made. The court also noted the support Mr Hamilton had received from his sister, is that correct? Yes, your Honour. She was thanked for bringing to the court's attention the ongoing injustice of the situation. At the back of the room Lynne nodded.

'Pursuant to the outcome of that assessment process, Mr Hamilton,' said the judge, turning to Edgar, 'it is possible that you should prepare yourself for release into the community. Do you understand?'

'Yep. Yep, I do.'

SIX

Edgar was released a few weeks later from Silverwater remand centre where he had been held for the time leading up to the hearing. He was discharged into his sister's care. His presence was not required at court for the order to be made, and at midnight the screws said he could leave now or wait till morning.

'Wait till morning,' he replied, gripping his doona tightly.

He was still asleep when his door was opened and a voice said:

'See you later, Ed.'

'But I ain't ready. I gotta — I gotta —'

'You gotta get out of here. This cell's needed.'

* * *

In reception, he was given his old clothes which had come down with him on the truck. He saw that they were rags. The father's boots were stiff and white with age. So he finally left them there and walked out of gaol in his runners and his prison greens. The doona he left behind too — someone would make good use of it. In his pocket he had the standard one week's dole money, plus the savings from his work in textiles when he had been in the Main (minus contributions made to victims' compensation).

Outside in the sunshine Lynne and I stood under a gum tree, leaves all about us on the footpath. Mum's blouse was green, but somehow it was a colour Edgar had not seen for a long time, unless it was the cut of the cloth. Inside her clothes she was as frail as a stick. She kissed him on the cheek. He could not remember anyone doing that before. When he glanced at her out of the corner of his eye, he saw again the resemblance to his mother, the same stoop to her shoulders, the way she held her hands. It wasn't really the mother, just her lingering shadow. He gave my suit a considered glance.

'I left the doona.'

'It must be pretty thin by now.'

Lynne had some new civilian clothes for him as they had arranged, jeans and a smart shirt, a pair of new boots. She hoped they weren't too small. The

Sydney weather was muggy, so he tied the jumper about his waist. He could not believe the noise and speed of the traffic along Silverwater Road. How fancy all the cars looked.

He waited for me to open the door for him. It wasn't locked. He had lost the habit of opening doors. We hadn't driven far. We needed petrol. I took him into a restroom at the service station to change. He jumped at the clarity of his reflection in the mirror. I was startled to see the great cicatrices on his chest. He changed quickly.

'What happened to your chest?'

'A flea bite me.'

'Must've been a pretty big flea.'

'Don't worry, I bite him back.'

He left the prison greens lying on the floor. When we returned, Mum asked:

'What do you want to do?'

We had a full tank. We could go anywhere. A hundred thoughts must have run through his mind. In the frenzy of impulses some of them slowed down enough for him to see them: What did he want to do? He wanted to rage, to smash, to devastate. He wanted to kill someone, but he dare not say that. He had to get his bearings. It was a world without fences.

'Eat ice cream, I reckon.'

So we drove to a shop where Lynne bought ice creams. Then she used her mobile phone to confirm their reservation at a city hotel. Edgar had never seen a mobile phone before, and didn't want to show that he was afraid of it.

The great buildings frightened him as we drove deeper into the city. Edgar couldn't believe how fast I was driving, although we were moving no faster than the traffic around us. I found myself driving extra carefully, as if there was a new mother with a baby in the back. Lynne pointed out all the latest developments she thought might interest him. The harbour sparkled, as it does, under a perfect sky. I looked in the rear-vision mirror at the miracle that was my uncle sitting in the back seat.

Why didn't all those boats on the water just crash into each other and sink?

Eventually we arrived, checked into the hotel. Nothing swanky, but comfortable. His first night of freedom — she wanted him to be comfortable. Edgar offered her the money in his pocket. It was all plastic. He didn't understand it.

'Is this all they gave you?' she said, handing it back. 'How are people supposed to make a clean start with this? This wouldn't pay for a good night at the pub. They want people to fail.'

'Sorry. Bought some Paddle Pops.'

'It's not your fault. It's them. They like recidivism. They encourage it.'

Edgar enjoyed the elevator very much. The doors opened by themselves. Once inside the suite, he did not want to leave. The room was enormous. Edgar could not believe that they would just give away all the things he found there: soap, shampoo, biscuits, little mini-cheeses. He had never seen anything like it. We ordered in dinner. Lynne did not hide her surprise.

'I thought you would want to go out and drink a skinful of beer and pick a fight with someone.'

Edgar had never tried beer. He had had some rum once, but it was nothing special. It had burned his whiskers. We sat by the window looking out at the city skyline. The cranes on top of the skyscrapers. Pigeons swirling. Not a patch of grass in sight. Lynne swallowed a great number of pills with her tiny meal, then went to the bathroom where I knew she was giving herself a subcutaneous injection of Neupogen. He didn't ask what the pills were for. He knew.

Nor did he want to go out after dinner.

'Where would we go?'

'Anywhere, anywhere!'

She could go out if she wanted, he offered. Lynne laughed, and he realised it was the first time he had heard that sound. She was too old for nightclubs.

'Tony might take you.'

No, he would not. I made some weary noises. He told her that he didn't think he would ever get to sleep, the bed was too big. What did people do in such big beds? He was happy just to sit and watch telly, to wander from room to room. Was he allowed to go into the hallway? Up and down in the elevator?

After dinner I made my excuses and left. Uncle Ed was free. I gave him my business card.

He did sleep. He pushed the bed against the wall and tried to rearrange the furniture in the room like his cell. He slept his usual thirteen hours, and in the morning he ate an enormous continental breakfast, before Lynne insisted that he have a bath. What an experience that must have been.

They spent the day and the next night and most of the following day together. They went to Bondi Beach and paddled in the shallows. The waves buffeted his legs and splashed his rolled-up trousers. The sea spray like nettles on his face. Then Edgar asked if they could leave because there were too many topless girls lounging about on the sand, and he thought it must have been because they knew he was just out of gaol.

'How would they know?'

'Ain't it splashed all over me dial?'

He felt himself burning. They trudged across the sand.

'That side of things must have been very difficult.'

'Well, I ain't too fond of eggs.'

He did not explain his hard laughter, shaking the sand out of his new boots.

Lynne told him all about the halfway hostel she had arranged, called Langwith House, which he could move into, if he wished. He would at least have a roof over his head. She gave him the keycard to an account, which contained a substantial amount of money, some of it left over from the sale of the property. And she taught him how to use the automatic teller machines. Together they went to Social Security, organised his registration, established which benefit he was eligible for. Edgar signed his name.

After lunch the last day, she spent a long time in her room packing her case, while Edgar gazed out the window. When she came out she said that Edgar could either choose to stay here, go to the halfway hostel, or find somewhere cheaper. It was up to him now.

Edgar did not like that word, *choose*.

He said, 'It sound to me, Lynne, like yer leavin'.'

'I've got to, Ed.'

'I din't think too much about it,' he said. 'I reckoned maybe I could come and live with you.'

Lynne looked at him sadly. Suddenly in his flesh Edgar knew, the way she moved, that she was in constant pain.

'My husband, Barry, would never permit it. It was the last straw getting him to agree to this.'

'He reckons I'm guilty?'

'He thinks I should be thinking about my health. And about our marriage. My cancer has returned, Ed. And Barry reckons I should think about myself, for a change. He's a good man. And maybe that time has come. I thought I'd been doing that all my life, and now I find perhaps I haven't; raising a family, supporting a husband. But Tony's an adult now, and you *can* manage, Edgar.'

'He reckons I'm guilty?' Edgar repeated.

'It doesn't matter what anyone believes.'

'What do you believe?'

'Again, it doesn't matter. I have to leave because I have to have another operation.'

'You reckon I killed that bloke?'

'Would I have slept here in these rooms if I thought that?'

'I din't kill no one but that poor dorg. I seen people die in the slot, but I din't care nothing for 'em.'

For a moment he looked steadily at her.

'Eddy, Eddy, little brother. You're free now. That's all that counts. You mustn't take that for granted. I don't think it's going to be easy but you've got to promise me that you won't go back to gaol.'

Beyond the window a world of light and splendour.

'I reckon I'll try.'

Edgar looked at his feet. Felt the hot nettles in his eyes.

'See you, Edgar.'

And she shook his hand, formally, as she had at the prison, before wheeling her case behind her and stepping into the elevator, smiling weakly back at him as the doors, all by themselves, slid shut.

Edgar stayed in his hotel room for three more days. He ordered up his meals on the phone, looking out the window at the constant motion of the city. All those people marching about, their destinations firmly in mind, bustling hither and yon on important business. All those people not in gaol. All those people trying to be good.

He went up in the elevator before he went down. Such a fun ride, and for free! Though now it was contaminated with abandonment. The doors opened by themselves on the empty space in the foyer. He approached the desk to check out, but the receptionist told him that the bill had been paid by Tony Tindale.

I keep trying to imagine him coping with the streets; the dilemmas he faced. He hadn't been outside for ten minutes when a hungry-looking beggar asked him for money to buy food. The beggar reminded him of someone, but whom, he couldn't recall. No, that was silly. The chances of him knowing anyone were — Edgar reached into his pocket and pulled out one of the newfangled plastic notes, the value of which he did not know.

'Thanks, mister!' the beggar said, scurrying off.

Edgar wandered aimlessly. He saw someone else he thought was Yema. It was not, but it made him think that one day he might bump into Yema again. What would they talk about? The good old days in gaol? He did not want to be reminded of gaol. The sound of trucks and jackhammers, of industry and commerce, assailed him. He gazed in awe at skyscrapers. The limited sectors of the divided sky. He hurried past the fashion boutiques changing their naked mannequins in the windows.

They made him hot and bothered. When he was hungry he stopped and bought some of the most exquisite-looking fruit from a stall on the side of the street. He did not know what to choose, only that he would never eat another pear again. The city was astonishing. And the women! High heels perplexed him. How did skirts work? He gave away more money to beggars, or to people who looked like beggars. Seeing his reflection in store windows he found a strange pride in the clothes he was wearing.

He looked up at the building he stood outside. It matched the number on the business card Tony had given him. He double-checked. He was good with numbers. He showed the card to a passerby who confirmed that, yes, this was the address. Edgar went up in the elevator.

The receptionist paged me to say, in a preposterous tone of voice, that someone who called himself *Uncle* had arrived. My shameful blood ran cold. He was looking at the fish in the foyer, tapping the side of the tank. I knew how much our receptionist hated that (there was a sign, which read: *Do not tap the glass*).

Edgar did not want anything in particular, he had just turned up. Everyone in our office was trying to eavesdrop on our muttered conversation. It was at this point that Mr Pennington returned from a meeting with the partners.

'Mr Hamilton, how splendid to see you.'

He shook Edgar's hand and was all brusque and businesslike, until Edgar asked old Penno how much was his suit? There was some discussion about the cut of the cloth.

Later Pennington summoned me to his suite.

'Tony, we can't encourage convicted criminals to loiter around the office.'

'I understand, Mr Pennington. He just arrived unannounced. I don't think he wants anything.'

'He makes Mrs Argyle nervous, having someone with a serious criminal record —'

'I believe there is enough evidence to overturn the conviction.'

'Not through this office, Tony.'

I looked at him.

'I would do it myself.'

'Mark my words, Tony, that man is as guilty as sin.'

'I don't believe that, Warren.'

He gave me a peculiar glance which seemed to suggest I was not the golden boy their good faith in me had augured, and perhaps I felt that too.

'Be that as it may, Tony, be that as it may. Am I to understand,' he continued, 'that your uncle wanted to buy my suit?'

The next day he was back. I quickly ushered him out of the foyer and downstairs for a bite to eat. We found a booth at a café I do not usually frequent. When he couldn't make up his mind I ordered for him.

'What do you want, Edgar? This can't go on.'

He could not answer me. He didn't know. The world outside was a daunting prospect. There were so many decisions to make. Too much choice. Being good gave him a headache. Then he made the longest speech I had ever heard him make:

'At least when I was in gaol, things were going good. I got fed regular. I got me some new teeth. I got a nice haircut. I got the bottom bunk. Even learned how to write me name. People talked to me. I had some friends. I knew how to stay alive. Out here I don't know nothing. Out here people just want money off me.'

The waitress brought our lunch. He tucked into his focaccia sandwich with gusto. All he knew he had to do would be to smash a window. His problems would be over. Do something that would keep him inside for a long time. Kill someone, maybe. I found myself reprimanding him like a child.

'Edgar, no. That wasn't the promise you made to Lynne. You've got to do your best not to think about killing anybody.'

Was I actually saying this?

'But Lynne went away and I'm on me own.'

'She's sick. She's dying. Don't you understand that? You've got to leave her alone. Tell me, where have you been staying?'

'I just walk.'

'What about that hostel she organised?'

'I lost the bit of paper.'

'I can fix that.'

'Tony,' it was hard for him to say, 'I don't like the city too much. I don't like bein' indoors. I just like to walk.'

'Edgar, you have no parole restrictions, you can go wherever you like. You can even go back home.'

'Wagga?'

'Well, the house is gone.'

'But the river?'

'The river would still be there, yes.'

I am ashamed to say that it suited me very well for him to reach this decision under his own steam. I was afraid that the next thing he might want would be to come home and meet Emily. In fact, Emily herself had suggested that Edgar and Pennington come around for dinner to celebrate our victory. An idea I deflected with stony silence. An idea which made me ashamed of my shame. This, this moral fortitude, is what Edgar had sensed missing from my life. And I knew he was right.

The next day he returned. He tapped at the fish tank. The partners all locked themselves in their offices. I took him to lunch again. This time to my usual restaurant. I needed to teach myself to like him. Trudy, the waitress, stared at us and, frankly, I stared back. We talked of ordinary things. The weather. If it was compulsory to give money to buskers. I allowed him to walk me back to the office; ride up in the elevator with me.

'If I wanted ter leave the city, how'd I go about it?'

I gave him directions to Central railway station. I even gave him a hundred for the fare, though I knew he had plenty of money. And I even closed the door behind him, and closed my eyes to Mrs Argyle's disdainful pity.

'If he calls again, shall I tell him you're out?'

I turned back to her.

'No.'

SEVEN

So Edgar walks. A destination in his legs. How must he feel? He crosses the streets only at traffic lights. He buys a hamburger and puts the papers in a bin. Is it possible? Is it possible for him to be good? If he stays here much longer he might be forced to neck someone. Eventually he sees the station, a train slowing behind the brick facade. The homeless with their spattering of coins laid out on cloth. Inside the high-roofed station a small city thrives, the sandwich stalls, the pub, the newsagency with so many magazines in the window. He sits and thinks about his actions for a long time. Some decisions are not always immediate. Delay is also a form of choice. He can, if he wishes stay here and live like these railway vagrants, sifting charity from peak hour. Make do.

A security guard wanders past and looks at him, but Edgar is doing nothing wrong. He is a law-abiding citizen.

When he thinks through all the decisions he feels are in his power to make, he goes and gazes at the flickering monitors showing the destinations and departure times. He forces himself to concentrate. He cannot see the letter he wants leaning like a stack of windblown trees. He stands patiently in the queue until it is his turn to approach the ticket window.

'I want ter go ter Wagga.'

'That's the Melbourne service, which has already left. Unless you want to go overnight, you'll have to come back in the morning. I'd advise that you pre-book.'

So Edgar pre-books, calmly taking out the wallet Lynne has bought him and selecting cash like an old hand. The man behind the window even gives him some change.

He returns to the railway station early the next morning. He studies the timetable closely. Having already purchased his ticket, yes, here it is in his new wallet, he finds his way to the designated platform.

And here is the train. And here is his carriage. And here is his seat. He verifies it with the conductor to make sure. He sits in his seat for over an hour. He doesn't want to miss this one.

The rhythm of the wheels is soothing. After they have rattled through the suburbs he is able to sleep comfortably through town after town, through the undulating hills slowly flattening towards the Riverina, and the flatlands beyond. His new possessions — a backpack and sleeping bag — are in the rack above his head. When they arrive at the big town the conductor wakes him up and calls him 'sir'. Edgar is amazed to be there so soon. Imagine how long, he thinks, it would have taken if he'd walked.

The light is as familiar to him as milk. He watches the train pull out and feels no sadness. It is just a train. He walks out of the station and stands looking at the main street. They have made some changes to the streetscape, but he recognises it well, like a dream. Cast-iron crows sitting on the street signs. Ha ha. The buildings much smaller than he remembers. He makes another choice and finds his way to the supermarket. The whole façade has changed, its entrance is now via a mall, which could be anywhere, replete with cafés and bakeries. There are twenty cash registers busily pinging away with the energetic sounds of profit. He recognises none of the checkout people. Nor is there any sign of his nemesis, Mr Ashcroft. Perhaps Mr Ashcroft is in gaol? Edgar is anonymous. No one resembles anyone else. He selects a trolley from the stack. He is blending in. He makes decisions about what he would like to eat that day, and the next day and over the following days and weeks. It is lucky they print pictures of tomatoes on the tins of tomatoes, beans on the bean tins, fish on fish. He buys matches, a can opener, a camp shovel from the hardware section, toilet paper, spare shirts, juice — he is being resourceful. This is planning for the future. He selects different brands and, holding them at arm's length, compares the pictures on the labels. On the basis of this he makes decisions. In aisle eighteen he comes across a wall of canned dog food towering to the ceiling. Ah, so this is where it all came from.

He gains a great deal of satisfaction from filling his trolley, then realising he does not have room for it all in his backpack, has to put half of it back. This oversight embarrasses him and he promises himself that next time he will not make the same error. He stands in line. He waits his turn. He selects a bill from his wallet and, when the girl still holds out her hand, selects another. Ping and ding go the till. She pours the change into his hand. She does not talk to him, so he does not talk to her. The transaction is complete. He has done it.

When he is organised he follows the main road west out of town. No one recognises him. He averts his eyes as he passes the hospital. The knee-high fences. The sprinklers. The golf course still brown and barren. When the suburbs finally disappear behind him he jumps the fence and begins to walk cross-country to the south. This, at long last, is what he has been waiting for. The smell of the grass, the sound of his feet swishing through it, the feel of it against his legs, all make his skin tingle into goose flesh. It is a sensation, in his skin and in his mind, that he does not have words to explain. It seems to stretch before him forever. He imagines a dog at his side coming to life in the grass.

His legs feel good. His muscles stretching pleasantly, the backpack hanging heavy on his shoulders. He is still fit. He feels as though he could march on like this forever. Once he sits down under his new hat in the long grass. He eats half a packet of biscuits and four apples. Then he marches on. Lynne is right. The old house has been sold. When he comes to the rise that overlooks the shallow dish scooped in the earth he sees that it has completely disappeared. The shed is gone. Even the old peppercorn tree. The fences dividing his land from Dungay's have also vanished. The weeds too have vanished. As far as he can see, there stretches a lush green sea of wheat. The horizon ripples. He cannot tell exactly where the house has stood. Even the old driveway is covered. He walks a few circles in the wheat, like a dog smelling its own lost scent. He walks through the wheat, and continues to walk. On the far rise of the earth dish he sees again the familiar lion-shaped silhouette of the Rock. Kengol. It is as familiar to him as a dream. He heads for that; his eyes on it like a wall. The only trace of his history left. Without such history, suddenly, he does not feel bereft at all, no no no, he feels free. Free and confident in the new world.

He learns the hard way that Dungay has now installed electric fences around his empire. It is another sensation he finds difficult to describe. The paddocks under his feet are like carpet. Perfectly ploughed. The heads of wheat whispering in the breeze. Grass seeds cling to his clothes. There is not a cloud in the sky. It is late afternoon when the grass thins and gives way to the bush, which thickens amongst boulders, telling him he has reached the Rock. In the little township, along the power lines, not a starling has moved, not a leaf has fallen since he last stood on this spot outside the butcher's. The same displays in the dusty windows. He skirts back out of the town and, crossing the shale slopes, begins the slow ascent. It isn't a mountain, it can't be called climbing. He sees the place amongst the she-oaks where the fox mauled him, and examines the boy he was once, crouching there in that spot. The boy turns, or Edgar's memory of the boy turns, their eyes meet. Then the boy that is Edgar raises his arm and seems to point further up the track. Wind sifts the trees. Does that boy exist outside his mind? The fox? Do any of his dogs? He rolls up his sleeve and looks at his arm. There is still a pale, faded scar. A scratch, amongst the newer ones. He walks on.

An hour later he makes it to the top, panting, not as fit as he thought. The view is still the same. Rectangles of bare earth alongside rectangles of sprouting green. Young wheat or yellow squares of canola. Or great coils of hay rolled up like snails. Parallelograms of stubble yet to be ploughed under the common denominator of the earth. It is like a great patchwork blanket he cannot see to the edges of. Around him on the hillside a recent fire has blackened many of the trees descending along the lion's flank. The black scars against the blue sky. Where will the crows hide now? Why, anywhere.

He finds he remembers the shapes of some of the rocks.

On the highway below he sees the ants of cars moving along. He climbs along the ridge, which also has the familiarity of a dream. There is no path, it is all overgrown — but Edgar knows the route where it dips down along the western side away from the road. Way below, to the right, he sees sheep the size of aphids. Fletcher could have come this way or climbed the ridge from the southern end, his own backpack weighing on his shoulders. He sees the shiny round coins that are dams reflecting the copper sun. Plenty of water, if he cares to climb down to it. Crows circling, their calls miaowing on the breeze.

He reaches the first of the hidden caves. There is no one waiting for him. Of course not. Although he knows the ridge intimately, he cannot say he remembers this particular cave, of the six or seven burrowing into the ridge. Why hadn't the boy he once was found this interesting? In gaol they sometimes called him a caveman. He knows how to live in a cave. He has survived. He puts down his things and builds a fire at the mouth and rolls his sleeping bag out on the ground. It is only marginally harder than the prison bunks he has grown so used to. The cave is about five times the size of a cell. He cooks meat over the coals of his fire and eats with his knife and fork on a tin plate. To the west the lights of only two homesteads glimmer in the distance. If he'd bought candles he would have been able to work at night. Should have thought of that. He has a ton of food in his backpack. He is a caveman with a credit card. Money in his pocket. If he runs out he might go and ask Dungay for a job. Wouldn't that old bastard get a shock at this bewhiskered ghost from the past. And if not him, then the next farmer, or the next. He doesn't even need the money. When he grows thirsty he will suck stones. What he needs, he decides, is a dorg.

Towards dawn a bushrat or some creature scampers over him. He wakes with a start. The fire is out, but still warm beneath the ash. Ducks are landing on the dams way below. He takes the camp shovel and begins to dig. Towards the back of the cave the dirt floor is shallow and he soon strikes rock. The mouth of the cave is deeper. He digs all day, piling the dirt up to one side — stopping to eat, then digging again — moving the pile from one side to the other so he can get beneath it. He places the smaller rocks aside and thinks they will do well for a wall to keep out the wind. He finds he has increased the headroom of the cave considerably. The smell of freshly turned earth fills his senses.

I still picture him up there — he is doing what he can for Sophie. Sophie had been kind to him. Or was it Ivy? One of them had been kind to him. He scrawls the first letter of her name in the dust, like the swoop of a bird in flight. At dusk he cooks his meal and sleeps and wakes at dawn to continue. He knows he has a problem with the rats, but that is something to set his mind to.

He is soon sweating again and, in time, has turned over most of the soil and shale in the cave, resting only when he uncovers a single, splintered bone. It is thin, like a penny whistle. There is nothing else. No small skull. He cannot even tell what sort of a bone it is. It might simply be a kangaroo's. Perhaps they are scattered, piece by piece, in the other caves? Perhaps they have been carried away by foxes? Well, he has plenty of time. He will excavate them all. He will dig for Sophie until he finds her. He is remembering his girl. He sits on his haunches by the dead coals at the cave mouth, his hands black with soot and earth and ash. The sweat on his face dusted and grey. He raises the smooth bone to his face and smells it, running it gently across his cheek, as the unseen sun behind the ridge slowly lights the great wide paddocks stretching away from him to the west. He watches as the sun picks out details he cannot have seen even a moment before, illuminating the expanse of land and all it contains and all his eye can apprehend.

Acknowledgments

While some of the incidents in this book are loosely based on anecdote, it is essentially a work of fiction. Several people have given me helpful and generous feedback at critical stages of this manuscript's development. I wish to thank Philip Dodd, Deb Westbury and particularly Peter Bishop for reading various versions of the story and making useful suggestions. An early draft of the book was written at Booranga Writer's Centre in Wagga Wagga where it was important for me to get the colour of the grass right. Thanks to David Gilbey for making me feel comfortable there.

In particular I would like to thank Linda Funnell of HarperCollins for her astute vision and critical eye in bringing Edgar's world to fruition. Her structural suggestions were pivotal in pulling the story into focus. The crucial phase of the manuscript's evolution took place at Varuna Writers' House. The ten days I spent there under the Varuna Award for Manuscript Development program were critical. I would also like to thank Judith Lukin-Amundsen whose precise eye for detail and editorial suggestions were invaluable. Finally I would like to thank my family for their support and love, which I return with deep thanks — Barb, Olivia, and Eamon.

Celebrating New Writing

THE VARUNA AWARDS FOR MANUSCRIPT DEVELOPMENT

These unique awards are for new or emerging writers of prose fiction or narrative non-fiction.

Each year the Varuna Awards offer five writers the opportunity to develop their work with a HarperCollins senior editor at Varuna — the Writer's House in the Blue Mountains of New South Wales. The awards aim to give practical assistance to new writers to bring their work to publication.

Applications close at the end of October each year, and the residential intensive takes place the following April.

For more information visit:

www.varuna.com.au/awardsformanuscriptdevelopment.html

Past winners include:

Denise Young *The Last Ride*
> Winner, NSW Premier's Awards UTS Award for New Writing, 2005; Shortlisted, South Australian Festival Awards for Literature, 2005

Robbi Neal *Sunday Best*
> 'One of the books of the year — I devoured it' *Australian Women's Weekly*

Penelope Sell *A Secret Burial*
> Shortlisted for the Kiriyama Award

Rebecca Burton *Leaving Jetty Road*
> Shortlisted, Older Readers category, Children's Book Council Awards, 2005

Ian Townsend *Affection*
> Shortlisted, Best First Book Commonwealth Writers Prize, 2005; Shortlisted, Victorian Premier's Awards for Fiction, 2005